The Body of This

andrew mcnabb

The Body of This

"Their Bodies, Their Selves" was previously published in *The Missouri Review*, Summer 2006. "Bride of Christ" was previously published in *Relief: A Quarterly Christian Expression*, Winter, 2007. "To Jesus's Shoulder" was previously published in *Not Safe, But Good* (Best Christian Short Stories, 2007.) (Thomas Nelson/WestBow). "The King of the Tables" was previously published in *Fierce with Reality*: An Anthology on Aging, NorthStar Press, 2006. "Herbert Wenkel Was Not Your Average Man" was previously published in *Rock & Sling*, Volume III, Number II, December 2006. "Extraordinary Whiteness" was a Many Mountains Moving, Prize Winner, 2006 Short Fiction Contest, Stolen Island Review, (University of Maine, Orono,) 2006. "Dead Man Walking," was previously published in *Words & Pictures Magazine*, Fall 2006. "Shed Drinker" was a Perigee: A Journal of Art, 2nd place, 2006 Short Fiction Contest Winner."

— — — — — — — — — —

Library of Congress Cataloging-in-Publication Data

McNabb, Andrew.
The body of this / Andrew McNabb.
p. cm.
ISBN 978-1-934866-05-4
1. Spirituality--Fiction. 2. Short stories, American. I. Title.
PS3613.C5855B63 2009
813'.6--dc22
2009001977

The Body of This

andrew mcnabb

For Sharon

toc

The Architecture of Things

I.

To John Thomas's mind, architecture didn't relate exclusively to the form and shape of buildings, but to the form and shape of everything. For example, he knew that it was their physical forms that had brought him and Aoife together; and he also knew that it wasn't because either of them possessed overwhelming physical beauty, but that their respective flaws were comparable—some might say, complementary—and that none couldn't be overlooked.

Her form, though, often made him wonder what made a woman with a small waistline and large breasts and full lips and a pear shaped bottom the best of what was to be desired? And why did a dimpled behind and small flat breasts and ill-defined calves represent something less than perfect? Whatever the detailed answer was, in short, it was human. Human? But what did that mean? That it couldn't be helped?

Some might say beauty is in the eye of the beholder, and that might be true, but John Thomas would say it's in the mind, and it's in the fingers. A man has needs, the saying goes, and when the mind triggers the body so that blood rushes to his penis, those small flat breasts and that big dimpled behind and those ill-defined calves could actually look quite nice. But even more than that, to the human fingers those parts were all covered by the same thing, flesh, and when your eyes were closed, flesh on one feels pretty much the same as flesh on the other. The substance beneath that skin might be different—one posterior might consist of more of that visually-valued muscle mass, another, more fatty tissue—but it was the job of the fingers simply to feel, and in each case what they felt was exactly the same: the epidermis.

But finally, thought John Thomas, and perhaps most importantly, when it came to physical feeling, in that ultimate act of human contact, that cavern into which the penis is inserted is essentially a piece of hardware and can, by no realistic man's definition, be considered a thing of beauty; and in his experience, which was not record-breaking, but hardly inconsiderable, all of those he had had experience with looked and felt approximately the same.

II.

But to stay together, the architecture of a relationship needs to be on firm footing. And because one measure of a relationship is the intensity of physical contact, imagine John Thomas's surprise when Aoife said, "I'm a virgin."

Like him, she was thirty. Wow. So what were you supposed to think about when you heard news like that? His thoughts, for a moment, went to the fact that that bit down there was still intact. But that bit was just a line of skin, a physical representation of an idea, really. What was more compelling was imagining all those years of her slapping hands away, of pulsating down there, being kept awake at night, of going quiet when the girls talked about their escapades.

At first, Aoife's ardent Catholicism was a curiosity he indulged, an eccentricity he found no different than if she had had a thick series of tattoos running up and down her arms, or a lifelong collection of Asian Barbies—amusing, peculiar, and something he didn't want for himself. But it ended up defining the both of them anyway.

It was confusing the way she wouldn't let him penetrate her but would wrap herself in all sorts of unusual positions to make him climax, each more lurid and depraved than the next; and then, not more than an hour or a day later, she'd have no problem going up and sticking out her tongue to receive her Christ.

Long after the newness had worn off, and shortly after a fight about what they were doing, where they were going, and after a series of news bits from friends who were advancing in careers, getting married, having babies, a particularly heated sexual episode occurred that needed to go somewhere further. Aoife got herself down on all fours. When he moved right in she stopped him.

"No, higher," she said.

He complied. That was a different bit of hardware, for sure.

When they were done, she sobbed, and he said they wouldn't do that again. He said he loved her. And after a half hour of lying there and feeling like he really did, he said, "Why don't we just get married?"

And so they did.

III.

By no means should the architecture of buildings be discounted. Bodies needed to be protected, of course, but it wasn't just that; being inside the proper architecture, immersed in a space and surrounded by thoughtfully designed details could provide a feeling that everything would be okay. Except that maybe it wouldn't; if you were Aoife, at least. She said she tried to live her life as if material things were fleeting, and John Thomas couldn't disagree that that was the case, but he also made the point that those things were still a component of this here life, just be sure to not let them rule you.

And that was the reason they finally settled on Portland. You could buy a house more cheaply there than you could in many other places. Not that they were in a position to do so just yet. But for the here and now at least you could walk among the turreted peaks and the orangey brick facades they'd seen nowhere else, floating on the thought that if they searched hard enough they would find an interesting place of their own.

The first place they saw, however, was not one of them. It was part of Aoife's general view on life that good things should be saved for. That's why she was always carrying around that damn calculator. When they found themselves standing in front of a three-decker on Montreal Street in the East End, John Thomas could see her clutching the calculator in her pocketbook, and he wasn't surprised when she said, "I could live there."

He didn't respond. And they didn't go in. He tried to tell her that he didn't need to see it to know what was already there. If the floor inside the front door was not covered by a worn red carpet and the walls by a shiny brown paint job, then peeling linoleum and fading flowery wallpaper would surely be the case. A wasted ten-speed would be tethered to the stairs, or maybe a child's plastic bike just left, forgotten until the next time. Three metal mailboxes, names scratched in and out, scattered take-out menus on the floor, an empty bottle of Diet Coke in the corner. And all of it wrapped in the smell of decades of comings and goings in a place that would never really be treated as home. So, despite the rent, no.

Moving on, all it had taken him to decide on the place they were now living was the cast-iron awning out front. It was a signal, a beacon. This building might be boxy and not so complex, but there were details here that you wouldn't find in any three-decker. The weathered mahogany door in the lobby, the black and white mosaic tile floor, the simple but well-polished banisters, the flowered plaster moldings. It even had a name: Northcourt. And after much debate, Aoife assented.

IV.

So with all of that now taken care of, John Thomas was remarking to Aoife just the other day how there were all sorts of things that enter and leave and surround our bodies, and she remarked with a smile that that was an unusual thing to think about. The smile was because she loved him, and she liked the way they talked about things like that a lot.

When it got to be her turn she made the point that how, finally, when certain things were in place, basic human needs met, what greatly formed the rest of you was what you ended up doing with your time. She, the music major, had just gotten a job as a secretary, and he took this as a nudge. He couldn't do the same class of job, and his new neck tattoo prevented discussion of it, but she wondered if maybe there were other opportunities that, if his creativity was competently engaged, could be worthwhile. He'd told her he'd think about that, and he did.

And so here they were, forming a life's rhythm together, indulging, somewhat, the conventions of what it took to exist and to be able to pay for things. They had been in that spot a month now, and just as he had said in selling the place to Aoife when they first saw it, it was nice being able to sit at the table by the window on a weekend morning and push down on a coffee press while you looked out at the little pocket park across the street. That was the case right now, except he was all alone.

As always, there were complications.

Aoife was in the bathroom peeing on a pregnancy stick. He had thought it might come to this. He didn't want her to be pregnant. He thought they should wait, and when he'd said that to Aoife, she'd replied she'd done all the waiting she could handle. Her sexual maneuverings had become more mundane, more functional, and she'd also said that they couldn't be stopped now and the act couldn't be covered in a plastic sheath for his penis.

The stream of urine coming from the bathroom was lusty, fueled by morning coffee, and perhaps by

Aoife's intense wishes; and despite the gravity of the impending outcome—he couldn't do anything about that—John Thomas let his mind settle on that little plastic stick, how it was something that you emitted the body's waste on and then how it would tell you if there was a tiny life growing inside you. My God, the architecture of that little piece, and the architecture of a woman's body, a little potential something taking root right up there in a woman's—in Aoife's—womb. All of that interconnected hardware.

The seconds dripped past, and then finally, with a flush, a verdict was upon them. The door opened and Aoife emerged. His eyes darted to her belly. Could something be living inside her? His eyes went to her face. She was smiling. But what did that mean? That she would soon start to grow, her belly expanding and distending, a little life inside her taking its own form and a shape?

As Aiofe kept coming, and with the sun at her back giving the appearance of flight, John Thomas had an overwhelming desire to talk, to remark that when a life was conceived wasn't it incredible that with each passing week body parts and organs would just appear and be added? And how, when complete, the tiny being would

Their Bodies, Their Selves

They had lived a clothed life. An accident had changed that. But what was an accident? It was just a word. There was no reason at all that what had happened shouldn't have happened. So many different things that happened were terrible or debilitating or life-ending, but who was to say that they should never happen? There were certain laws of physics that couldn't be flouted just because the consequences were terrible. That was the world. And speaking of physics, here the two of them sat, Drayton and Sarah Maguire, naked, wilted.

From his side he saw flesh; and from hers, she did, too. It was how they felt about it that was different, but she was coming around. She was the one who had started it, actually, though that had been unintentional. And with a swing of his head—the only action he was still capable of—it was now a daily ritual, his imploring her, and himself, to their natural state.

It had begun six months prior, on a Saturday just after four-thirty in the afternoon, the time each day when Dray would disappear to the bathroom for fifteen minutes of flushing solitude, when out came the noise. The noise. In this life—and, especially, in the daily consciousness of the old—there is the tremendous and unmistakable *Smack!* of the human skull on porcelain. There it was; and Sarah dropped her knitting.

Okay, how to continue? Let's continue with where they were. They were at their little beach cottage forty-five miles up the Maine coast from Portland. It was an unassuming little house in an area where development was forbidden. To get there you'd take the same road you took to get to the state park not far away. On that road there were just two opportunities to turn, the park and the Maguire's little dirt road. Travel up that dirt road through a forest so thick with pine it was nearly dark even at the height of day, and at the end of it, in the clearing, was their cottage among all the dunes.

A lifetime of memories, but so remote, their son had forbidden them from going there.

If you took the building just for what it was—one level, three rooms—and ignored the dunes and the puffins and the sea grass and the few small pine-treed islands just offshore you wouldn't have much. The shingled sides were drying up and salting away, the roof was solid but fading. And inside things were rudimentary. Maybe they had been lush at one time—Drayton's father, though Irish, had been one of the wealthiest men in the state, a bull and a ship-builder, and he'd built that salt-box as a retreat with his mistress—but now the propane stove and the pull-flush toilet were peculiar, unreliable. The structure was lucky to be standing at all, but because it had always been standing, as far as today's conservationists knew, it was allowed to stay, but not allowed to be worked on, which was fine with Drayton, if not so fine with his wife, his amends, perhaps, for developing up big swaths of southern Maine in pre-fab sub-divisions and run-of-the-mill golf courses that many said had changed the face of the state. Drayton wouldn't disagree, but his philosophy was give them what they want, and there had always been his own tiny little section of the state, the West End of Portland, to retreat to.

But back to the accident. If that was the word. Or maybe it was just life's gravity.

There were a certain few seconds between that *Smack!* and their discovery of each other when the immediacy of their thoughts summed things up perfectly. Sarah—eighty-one, genteel, Yankee Protestant daughter of a pulp and paper king, black sheep for marrying the Catholic though he was even wealthier than they, their children's Episcopalianism partially redeeming her—was up quickly, but still moving slowly, and was simply hoping she wouldn't find blood. To her—scarred from shingles, melanoma, three ungrateful children and an undiagnosed depression—life was winding down anyway, and a quick descent she was ready for, just let it not be too messy.

And then Dray, for his part—eighty-four, still wearing a bow-tie most days, still going to mens-only dinners at the club, still with the occasional idea of what plot of land to develop and why—sensing the little pool of blood by his ear, but feeling little else, could only think about one thing: what he'd left in the toilet. Sarah was going to see it. In all their years together, to his knowledge, she'd never seen anything he'd left behind, because he was assiduous in all matters of the body, and he could thank his good Kerry-born mother for that. And now Sarah was going to see that in the toilet, and she was going to see him, pants completely off, the way he'd been doing it lately so he wouldn't get caught up when he stood. But on came the footsteps, and the unmistakable twist of the door's tin handle. He closed his eyes and considered playing dead.

Sarah came in to a breathing silence. She maintained it, except for her little groan when she tried to lift him, as if he was a log that had rolled off one of her father's lumber trucks three generations ago. She was calm, as if this was just as natural as could be, and maybe it was. And yes there was blood, but not too-too much, she would just deal with it. And then Dray opened his eyes. All Sarah could do was turn.

"I'll call 9-1-1," she said.

When she returned she hoped she'd find something different. But no, it was just her husband's lower nakedness, pathetic and heavy and splayed on that cracking Macomber slate floor. His eyes were closed — for her benefit, she knew. It was a frozen moment. Then what came next, neither of them had expected.

"Drayton," she said. "Drayton."

Drayton opened his eyes to see her undressing. In all those years together there had never been a moment like this. Never had there been a romantic undressing. There had hardly been an incidental one. They each had snapshots and captions of bits and pieces of each other, the whole amounting to a composite of things maybe real, maybe not quite, and here now all that was ending.

Off came the sturdy black shoes, down came the gray wool skirt, the thick beige stockings, the heavy underwear, and over the head went the plain white cotton shirt. Out came the revealing heaviness of that sagging breast, pointing south to the melting of her inner thighs as if to say, There you are, and here I am. That is just you, and this is just me, and here is my pubic hair gone gray.

What had been in his eyes was now something else entirely.

When the paramedics came in, they found both of them naked. Sarah saw the looks they gave each other. She didn't care what they were thinking. She did it for her husband, she wanted to say. Except that she hadn't. At least maybe not entirely.

And now look at them. They were back at their beach house. It was August and it was dusk and their skin was tingly and warm in the uncharacteristic southerly Maine breeze. Outside that dilapidated cottage were the dunes and the puffins and the sea grass, and inside were the two of them, sitting across from each other, just looking, thinking.

Blemished

On that particular Sunday in late May, when the dogwoods lining Portland's streets had already gone and bloomed white, and now with half their petals browned and fallen to the brick, Thaddeus Karpinsky sat frozen under his cassock and surplice on the altar of St. Stanislaus church on the corner of Danforth Street and Emery.

Not unlike Thaddeus, St. Stanislaus was a plain-faced thing, small and boxy, with none of the grandeur of a typical Catholic tribute. There was a bit of stained glass but no marble at all. The walls were covered in faux-wood paneling. Hanging from the ceiling were yellowish light fixtures meant to look gold. And in the ultimate statement of something—cheap architecture? an unusual understanding?—Mass was said on the building's second floor.

How odd was it that when you walked up the few plain cement steps and into the church there was no blessed sanctuary to greet you, just a meager hall of faded tile and a ceiling held up by big thick beams? The only sense that this was a church at all was hanging from each of the side walls. Look to your left and Polish was the language, announcements and prayers, a poster of a fetus underlined by exclamations and harsh Polish letters, a picture of Karol Wojtiyla as the archbishop of Krakow; young, square-jawed and handsome. The right side mimicked the left except it was in English and the picture of Karol Wojtiyla was twenty years later, sitting hunched, the world's bishop.

And so it was on that day, when the air and warmth outside had signaled a deep and final change from spring to summer, that Thaddeus sat off to the side of the altar, a flaccid thirteen year old, shrinking under the Gospel reading; that morning he had woken up with a wet spot in his underpants. It had happened just once before. That time he had had a dream that a cat was scratching and pulling down below and then whoosh, he woke up gummy. And that time it could be ignored, or at least excused. But this time was different; the cat was a girl, someone he knew.

He couldn't look his parents in the eyes that morning. He had told them a while back he would be a Marian, just like Fr. Bednarek. He had wanted to rescue something falling. But forget it now with the way his mind churned on the strong thighs and the lifted bottom bubbling through the pants of that refugee girl, Nika. A priest! If he ever wanted to minister to anything it was her posterior, as ethereal as the Gloria, Gloria!

Could he have communion that day? He didn't want it. He had been asking for a sign, and that's what he had been given: a cat and a girl. So why not look out into the pews then, in her direction? Nobody could see what went on under his cassock.

So that's what he did, and what he saw was the biggest, roundest pimple he had ever seen, pink and raised and grotesque on her black skin. He held on tight to his chair, feeling that whole first floor beneath his feet sag. And then whoosh! His heart was filled again.

The Hunchback of Munjoy Hill

In the state of Maine, in the city of Portland, at the foot
of Munjoy Hill on Congress Street just east of the broad
new passageway known as Franklin Arterial, there was a
tailor's shop on the second floor of an old brick building.

At that moment in time—and in many other moments,
most moments—what was felt and seen inside and out
of Frank Iannone's now-defunct shop was dominated
by shape and color and form. First, the building; with
its elaborate masonry and composite cement-sculpted
porticos, with its looping, mullioned windows and its
faux neo-gothic peaks; but also—and especially—with its
limited use because of its stodgy staircases and smallish
spaces, its outdated systems and crumbling neglect due

to fifty years of it not quite *fitting*, it was targeted to be reworked and reframed into an exposed-brick idyll for baby-boomers from out-of-state. And its last remaining tenant would be evicted.

The tailor; standing, presently, at the window, up on his tip-toes behind a sheen of Genoan silk gone spotty and frayed from its own years of neglect. Short was now shorter, gone from five-foot-three to five-foot-even, those inches having dripped away over the course of one long decade, a bone and flesh IV, not gone forever but accumulating into a hump on his back. It contributed to his legend, Frank Iannone, the Hunchback of Munjoy Hill. Slumped, yet still looking up, and looking as if his days were powered by that curve, all his life and all his ambitions mixing and coagulating until they had calcified into one hard question: Where the fuck were they all coming from?

The they in a moment, but first, the fuck. Over the first eight decades of his life, curses from Frank's mouth could have been counted on his fingers and toes with the left foot gone untouched. But now that sum was broken in just about any ten minute span. Get to the fucking corner to get the fucking-fuck. What's in the goddamn toilet? Aahh shit-the-fuck. Fucker-fuck. Fuck it. Fuck.

And now, for the they. The they were Africans, black as the mid-summer eggplants he once grew in his pocket garden two blocks away. Not black American black, but black African black, that particular shade of unadulterated obsidian that was still easily discerned by having made a living with his hands immersed in colors and fabrics, his fingers and eyes expertly assessing each body's parts; and once he had even outfitted a visiting professor from Nigeria in his first real suit.

Those were the days, sitting behind his Singer, watching the world outside his window and now, here he was, shut in, closed off, humped, but still by that window, waiting for that next sighting of despotic beauty to keep him going, those stretched limbs, that cracked skin so dark against the snowy white, a question pursed on his lips. The fuckers, the fuck, where were they all coming from and why the fuck why?

Bride of Christ

Because, as a little girl, she tried to listen when it was said, All those who have ears ought to hear, Elsie McCain thought it could be the height of romance being the bride of Christ, even if He was a polygamist with all the nuns already out there able to stake that same claim—but with Him it would be different.

Her mother's predilection for images of that tortured, thorny Jesus—not the hanging, napping one—only told part of the story; what had really sparked it was the summer between sixth and seventh grades when between all the Judy Blumes and that one long Chronicle of Narnia came Englebert's *Lives of the Saints*. Never had Elsie suspected all of the little ones. She'd counted no fewer than twelve young virgins, some of them no older than she was, given away to kings and noblemen only to escape for the privilege of hiding in a cave to pray or to flee to some foreign country. One such little bit, Cecilia, even begged to be ripped to shreds by wild animals instead of being turned back, and how could you compare that to Margaret obsessing about her bra size in *Are You There God? It's Me Margaret.*

But that wasn't the least of it. Come September, it was Sr. Kathleen who made all the difference. She was the youngest nun Elsie had ever seen, before or since. And you couldn't hide that beauty behind hairpins and a habit. That was a God-given nose, upturned just enough to make the human eye want to stare, and those were big brown eyes like French chocolates, and behind those perfectly-formed red lips were teeth so straight and white it looked like an angel had dropped them in. You want sacrifice? There, you got it. And every day before school Elsie thought about St. Rose of Lima, who'd disfigured her face to rid herself of all vain attempts, half-expecting Sr. Kathleen to do the same to keep the boys from staring.

But then that next summer Elsie's path was changed for good. She went back to school that fall with breasts as large as any of the teachers' and all of a sudden, in those classrooms soaked with body odor and hormones, the main attraction was her. The occasional note sent her way had turned to a flood, a touch, an occasional grope. Billy O'Connor was that class's prize and they met out in back of the school every afternoon, Elsie tingling from the curiosity of Billy's tongue. It wasn't long before his hand was moving up the inside of her shirt—his prize. For a while she managed to block everything else out; until, finally, that painful, embarrassing fumble ended with her lying in bed that night draped in a rosary recounting all those little devout souls, married up to losing their lives so that they could save them, and Elsie promised the Lord if he kept her from being pregnant she would somehow, some way, find a way to die for Christ just like so many of them did, and what could be more romantic than that?

Fast-forward twenty-five years, and Elsie's dreams, in one form or another, were still alive. She was married, not to Christ, and not to Billy O'Connor, but to a man named Greg Parker. They had a child together, and though her breasts were as big as they'd always been, the little one had sucked the life right out of them, leaving her flat and dangling, but that

To Jesus's Shoulder

Charlie was always trying to do it some different way. Whenever he invited me for coffee it was never to one of those trendy spots downtown but to a place that most would say had no character for drinking coffee, like the canteen in the parking lot on Marginal Way where the coffee came scalding hot in spongy Styrofoam cups, or the seventh floor of the library over at USM where the coffee poured from a vending machine just inside from the double-door next to the elevator. And one time he even asked me to meet him at the 7-Eleven on Congress. We had an hour-long conversation just standing right there by the coffee pot, next to the Drake's cakes and the case of warm breakfast burritos.

And that was just coffee. There was the rest of Charlie to consider. Take the way he dressed, for example. I have no idea where he got his clothes. My guess is at Goodwill. Maybe that's not unusual, but what he wore was. It was always slightly frayed, and it was always colorful. He might wear red polyester slacks with a tartan shirt one time, and the next he might have an old gray suit coat over a lime green shirt so wrinkled you might think that was part of its design. Charlie would never say that he had a personal style, but I described him to himself one day as Delightfully Rumpled, and there was the nicest gleam in his eye over that.

And then there was the way he walked. He leaned back a tiny bit, as if he was going under the world's highest limbo setting. And his greetings. "How's the day?" he might say. Or, "How did it feel when you got up this morning?" Whatever he asked, it was always a surprise, and always, it seemed, intended to cause you to think about things in a different way.

But what was most unusual about Charlie was his questions. They could almost always be approached from two sides. At our most recent meeting Charlie wanted to discuss mail. He opened up the conversation by saying,

"Is there anything more satisfying than that moment right before you drop a piece of mail into the mailbox? Check the address. Check the stamp. Open the lid, drop the mail, and *Clink*, you're done! Voila! Another task completed!" He stopped, paused, and looked into my eyes. "But then there's the rest of life until that next mailing." I don't know anyone else who ever thought of things that way.

Now, no one can do everything unconventionally. You still have to live somewhere, and you still have to eat, and unless you want to live in something like a yurt on a Mongolian steppe or in a closet in an old abandoned house, and subsist on a diet of bark or stones, you have to figure out how to fit into the system, at least a little bit. So Charlie worked part-time at a trinket store selling Maine paraphernalia to tourists—"I'm a scrimshaw man!" he'd say enthusiastically—and he always had interesting ways to think about what he did there, and to describe the type of people he met. "Do you know what it takes to talk the tourist talk?" he asked me one time. "Time!" was his answer, and he went into a long discourse about the different ways that could go.

It wasn't that I waited for his calls, but I did look forward to them, mostly because I don't do things the way Charlie does them. And so when he called me last week and said, "To The Donut Cart!" I was excited to go. What would he tell me? How would he want me to deal with it?

It was a great spring day and I was happy to be out from work. I had been to The Donut Cart on many occasions and had always seen it as just that: a steel cart with a man standing inside, serving donuts and coffee through a small window. Thinking that the cart may be today's topic, I attempted to analyze it; it was rather unusual for a man to be standing inside a small tin cart, so small that he always looked unhappy and cramped. But the counter balance to that was the beauty of the surroundings. And that, in turn, got me thinking further; unlike all of the other places we had met—sandy parking lots, convenience stores, windowless cafeterias—this spot had a view. It was right up against Casco Bay, with nothing ugly in sight, just an unobstructed view of the water and the few small islands.

When I arrived at The Donut Cart, Charlie was already there. He looked a little more rumpled than usual, but no less colorful. Orange corduroy pants and a buttonless vest over a white T-shirt. And then another new view for me; his arms from his biceps down were exposed. They were so thin and white.

As always, he started right in. "Sit, sit. Two parts today. One, did you ever think that maybe it's not all that bad to suffer? And two, did you know—and don't just automatically say yes or no—but did you know that there is a prayer to the shoulder wound of Jesus?" He flashed one of those little cards that people sometimes leave behind in phone booths or on tables at diners.

All I could think about was not the answer to the question, but how it was a different type of question. Quite different than, "Quick! What are the ingredients in a traditional Sevillian bouillabaisse?" Or, "I'm glad you're here, now let's talk about how it feels to stand all day long."

Of course, I had no idea there was such a prayer as one to the shoulder wound of Jesus, but before I even had time to answer, he said, "The shoulder wound! Mon dieu!"

And then, as he often would, Charlie went into an amalgam of thoughts and notions about the topic, telling me it might help if I thought of my own shoulder, its function, it being a joint attached to a socket and secured by tendons, muscle and cartilage. "Hammer it down," he said, "with a great and heavy weight. Tear the flesh, boy!" He speculated that if there was a prayer to Jesus's shoulder wound, there must also be a prayer to the holes in His hands and in His feet and to the hole lanced in His side to ensure His death, but he didn't know for sure and that didn't matter anyway because what was most interesting about this prayer, he said, was that it was the result of an unrecorded suffering.

"What do you mean unrecorded?" I asked.

He flashed the card again. Someone named St. Bernard had a personal conversation with Christ after Christ died and St. Bernard asked Christ what his greatest unrecorded suffering was—and, of course, all I could think of was how St. Bernard asked unusual questions, just like Charlie—and then Charlie read a prayer that contained some of those very same words he used, like flesh and bones laid bare and the crushing burden of a cross. He huffed, and he sighed and he said, "Can you imagine all that? Unusual. Unusual. A prayer to a wound."

Yes, it was an unusual day. And then we just sat there for the longest time, silently, which was unusual in itself. In the past, he would always have at least one addendum, like, "So, which route will you take home tonight?" Or, "Now tell me again about the day you were born."

Instead, we just sat looking out at the beautiful scenery, the sun high overhead and the cool wind floating in off the water, the caustic Donut Cart brew maybe serving some type of purpose, tempering the surroundings, I guess, in light of the shoulder wound and the suffering we were now supposed to consider.

Finally, after quite a deliberation, Charlie said, with a great deal of levity, "To Jesus's shoulder!"

"To Jesus's shoulder," I replied. And, at least for that day right there, that was that.

I told her yes, I did, and I said, "What's wrong with it?" even though I knew what she thinks is wrong with it. She thinks that artists are crazy. She knows all about Van Gogh and how he cut off his ear, and then she probably looks at my work and says, My boy is going to cut off his ear someday, too.

So anyway, I like that old folks home so much that a little while ago I started painting it. I stand across the street from it with an easel. I don't care much for the people who stop and look. Most of them want to talk. The only reason I'm there and not in my room painting from a picture is to see how the building evolves, but I don't say that to them, though. That would sound so artistly, and I'm not into that, unlike many of the other students at art school. They all want to prove to everyone how artistly they are with how they dress and everything. I heard Professor Richards saying to another professor at the student art show something about the boastfulness of youth. They were shaking their heads, and it even looked like they were laughing a bit. You might never know at all that I'm an art student unless you saw me painting out there on the sidewalk, and the only reason I'm doing that is because I want to see the building breathe, and so that I can see some of the old folks in their rooms. A lot of them just sit and watch TV.

It's not that I want to just sit and watch TV all day long as the reason for wanting to almost die. I want to almost die because I wouldn't mind just living in a building like that and having nothing to do all day long. And in order to live there, you have to be very old. It would be a drag being so feeble, though. I think about that a lot when I'm thinking how I would really like to live there—on those days when I have tests or when I have to go to work—because then it makes me feel a little bit better about my own situation. I think to myself, Well, you've go to do all this other bullshit, but at least you don't walk with a cane, or at least you don't have to have someone pushing you around the block in a wheelchair.

A few weeks ago one of the old ladies came up to me while I was painting. I was surprised to see her up close because even though I've never talked to her before in my life I feel like I know her very well. She walks around the block every day. She may do it five or six times and it takes her like an hour. She always wears the same thing, these cheap gray pants and stiff shoes and an ugly old sweater. I'm always across the street so she doesn't walk right past me, but then on that day a few weeks ago she came across the street and I've never seen her do that before and I kind of knew she was going to come and talk to me. She didn't have much to say. She said, "Oh," to start off with when she looked at my painting. And I think she wanted me to say something back and so I said, "It's your building." When she said a few more things, all I could do was look into her mouth. She had really rotten teeth. They were all gray and brown, and she had a few whiskers on her chin. The whole time she was saying things I just looked at her and wondered what it must feel like looking like that, and then she walked back across the street and did her laps around the block. So I started to paint her as she walked around the block. I made her just as she was, which if my mother saw she would think was frightful and she would worry about me even more.

Ever since then I started painting some of the other people in the building, the people I could see. That's what I meant before when I said that I liked to paint the building out front and not from a picture, when I said the building was breathing. The breathing, though, was wheezy, just like that old lady, and just like the old man who always sits in his wheelchair outside. He has an oxygen tube in his nose and a little tank attached to the back of his wheelchair. That must suck. I want to ask him if he always has to wear that tube, or if it's just when he's outside.

But things like that don't make me not want to live there anyway. The building is kind of cool, which you probably wouldn't expect in a place for old folks. It's sort of angled and has little compartments; it's not just a rectangular building. It's a nice red brick, and it's new but it's kind of made to look old, and I think that's because most of the buildings in the area are brick but they really are old. There's one apartment in particular that I would like to live in, and there's a couple of reasons for it. One, it's on the top floor and there must be good views from there. And two, the guy who lives in there I think looks a lot like me, or at least how I think I might look when I'm old like that. He's very thin and at the same time he's tall. But maybe it's just the way he goes outside onto the little porch everyone has and sits there and stares out at the world as if everything just sucked. But what I like about it most is that he can go back inside and sit and watch TV and he doesn't have to do a damn thing until he dies. He's got a nice little couch, and they all have small kitchens, with just refrigerators. I think they must not be allowed to cook because they might burn the place down they're so feeble, but it's even better that way in my opinion because there's a dining room down on the first floor where they have all of their meals prepared for them. So I think that's what I'd like about living there the most, is that they don't have to do anything. They already did all the things in life they were supposed to do and now everything is all done for them, and they know it. All they have to do is breathe. So I guess that's also what I mean about liking to paint the building standing out front and not inside my dorm room with a picture, because I can see them just breathing and it's interesting to see what it's like when that's all you have to do. I think many people would disagree, but I think I would like life much better that way. Too much just sucks. And that's why I want to almost die. But it's going to take a long time to get there and so for now, I'll just be an artist instead.

To Be Married

The night—or morning, it was two a.m.—was filled with August steam. Wharf Street was a cauldron of drunken souls. The bars had let out and Dennis Cuinningham was off to the side with a girl named Monique. She had sprinkled something sparkly all over her so that her cheeks and her shoulders and that lovely patch of flesh just up from her... breasts... were alight like the nighttime sky.

She kept saying, "You're so cute!"

All Dennis could do was smile and laugh and keep talking. She was from Boston, and he was telling her about growing up on Prince Edward Island.

"Prince What Island again?"

"Ha ha—Edward."

"Edward. I like the way you say that, you're so cute!"

But he wondered was it cute that, just below his surface, floating in a moat of Guinness, was his recent year at The Monastery of the Precious Blood, in Cutter, New Brunswick, where the omnipresence of that massive, tortured likeness of Christ, thorned and dripping, still couldn't help him pray down his erection?

Their conversation led them to a different spot, the couch in his brother's apartment a few streets away. Those sprinkles sparkled even closer now, her breasts nearly resting on his arm as if it were a shelf. She had changed her exclamation to a question she kept asking—in an attempt at depth?—"But what do you want?"

Right then, with nowhere to go, and with nothing stopping them, he said, blurted, "To be married."

Yes, he realized, it was true. It was what he wanted. At least for that night, at least for the imprimatur. And with those twinkles on her chest shining so brightly, he could hardly make out the expression on her face.

It Look Like Dick

There are many great and ironic misfortunes. Into each life a number of them must fall. Muhammad Ali had a particularly keen one. No, not that Muhammad Ali—although he certainly suffered his own—but a different one, the one born into a small community of nomadic herdsmen in eastern Somalia; the one who, with his family, was chased all the way to Kenya, and then eight years later relocated half a world away to a small city called Lewiston in a place called Maine, where the most notable thing to ever happen was a boxing match between that famous Muhammad Ali and some poor soul named Sonny Liston.

It didn't take long for the five Alis to discover Muhammad's celebrity. "Muhammad Ali? There

was a boxer... and right here in Lewiston... and..."
And everywhere they went there was that picture—
Muhammad Ali, fist across chest, sinew exploding, a
triumphant scream as the crumpled Liston dropped to
the canvas like a buckshotted deer in the North woods.

"You gonna be like him someday?" he was often
asked with a smile.

Perhaps today was the day. It was hot dog day
at Lewiston High. And even at the age of fifteen,
Muhammad knew that if he had been born Omar
Omar or Hassan Ahmed life would be different, and
there was not a chance in Allah's paradise he would
be sitting there at the cool kids' lunch table, where his
nickname was Cassius.

So there he was in his corner, possessing all of
those ethnic traits in caricature—thin of head, narrow
of limb, bright and long of teeth—that fueled today's
fury, though he'd done what he could to cover himself in
that drooping uniform of American wannabe gangsta.
And in the other corner, across the lunchroom, was his
unwitting opponent, Miss Martino, who was nearly
twice his size, and who shunned the teacher's lounge to
eat with the students she so loved to be around.

And the purse for today's bout? At least for Muhammad it was the admiration of Jacqui Cyr, the queen of the table, and the daily wearer of a thong that pop-popped right up from the backside of her pants, doing much more than inkling those two pale half-moons of beauty; it was hard to reconcile how she could be walking the same halls as his two sisters, wrapped up in hijab and masar, their round chocolaty faces all anyone but their future husbands would ever see.

The lunch bell rang. Muhammad watched, waited.

A minute forty-six into it Martino left herself wide open, having a great and ironic misfortune of her own, that of loving food, but of hating bread, so having shed the bun, and having raised the naked dog to her lips at precisely the moment that Muhammad stood, pointed and swung with all his might:

"Ha-ha! It look like dick!" he yelled.

All eyes went to Muhammad, then to that other fighter, Muhammad's own Sonny Liston. Triumph, defeat, and that picture, recreated.

The King of the Tables

Glenn Miller's "Blue Rain" floats like a memory through the basement of St. Gregory's Church on Stevens Avenue. It's staticy, but it's gorgeous, and Frank can practically see young Glenn and his orchestra as if they were right there beside him, mouths blowing brass, Ray Eberle holding the mic, and Glenn's foot working it, tap-tapping the black and white tiled floor, so church-like, sealed by glossy wax and time… <u>Blue, blue rain, falling down my window pane</u>… sings Ray, setting an elbow fat with arthritis in motion, a humped back bounding back and forth, spotted hands afloat. Frank leans against one of the thick basement poles and takes in the scene, the dozen seniors preparing the hall for the weekly soup kitchen. It had been his idea, bringing in the old phonograph, and Father Mike hadn't objected, and now look at those old bones go… <u>But when you return there'll be a rainbow, after the blue, blue rain</u>…Inside it's 1942 again and outside it's early spring, still chilly and blue sky New England. Frank is wearing his best cardigan sweater and gray pants. And today will be the day.

Her name is Rose Breeley and there she is, sitting next to Mary Simmons, wrapping donated cutlery in scratchy napkins. He watches her hands, so delicate, the way she takes the fork and spoon, wrapping them carefully, lovingly… Today, tomorrow, sings Frank to himself, inserting his words into Glenn's song. Today, he would ask Rose to have tea, for tomorrow, at her home. His place just wasn't suitable. He'd recently moved into BonnyCrest, where the slogan was "Choice," which was supposed to mean all sorts of things, but when it came right down to it it just meant assisted living or unassisted. He was unassisted now but it wouldn't be that way forever. That morning he'd woken up soaked in his own urine.

But Rose Breeley wasn't nearly at that point yet. She was the youngest one there, just seventy and her husband had been a university professor, the famous kind, the kind who wrote books and went on news programs, and Frank knew Rose was not unsuitable for that type of man—so different from him, who'd had a career selling fasteners. Frank knew she lived in a big home on Vaughan Street in the West End. It was the one with the giant beech tree out front imported from Europe a hundred years ago with this day in mind, when it would tower over the house, the street, and Portland itself, its base as thick as a small truck. She kept up that house all by herself.

… And there's a blue star, looking down asking where you are… Frank moves on, heading for the supply closet, enjoying the music and the calm, the quiet before the rush of hungry bodies through the door, when the mood would sometimes change inside. "Come on, you scattered old fuck!" one of the men had said last week to Frank when his food hadn't come out quickly enough, and Frank had pretended not to hear him. They did it differently there at St. Gregory's. Each of the churches in town took one day a week feeding the hundred and fifty mouths, but St. Gregory's was the only Catholic one and the only one to serve the men and women, not have them wait in line. Father Mike had insisted on it. But there were more mouths now for some reason and the number of servers was dwindling. Hattie had died just last week. Frank had gone to elementary school with her. She crosses his mind now, but he pushes her away. He looks out over the scene again, the bodies bumping ever-so-slightly to the music, the lightness of it all, and he thinks how it wouldn't be so bad to freeze this spot in time. He lets his eyes go unfocused, as sweet Ray sings … <u>Then there'll be no more blue rain, just the sound of my heart's refrain, singing like a million bluebirds, after the blue, blue rain</u>…

***

Out in the back room, Frank gathers supplies and phrases a little conversation in his head. "Look at that Rose, The King of the Tables has us working side-by-side again." He envisions her laughing sweetly, and she would reply, "That King." It's how it had happened last week. Frank was the one in charge of assigning servers to tables and for the last month he'd made sure to put Rose on the next table over from him. When there was downtime, they would be close enough to chat. He spent all week thinking of things to say. Today, he would say,

"Say, Rose, how about a cup of tea some time? Yes? How about tomorrow?"

A knock at the supply room door startles him. "Frank?"

"Yup, just getting…" He grabs two big cans of tomatoes and emerges from behind the door.

Jerry, his best friend, is standing there. He's still solid, like Frank; but he's a half a foot shorter and has weathered time a bit better. Frank has a slight limp he covers up mostly by going slowly. Frank and Jerry had been together at Dumont Elementary, and then at the high school and then right into the military together, fought at the Battle of the Bulge side-by-side. Jerry married Doris and Frank married Anne. They were both gone now, and enough time had passed that Jerry could sometimes say with a smile, "Those ladies couldn't outlast us, could they, Frankie?"

"Everyone's at the back," Jerry says now. They gather at the back every week for coffee and a bit of conversation before the doors open.

Frank brings the cans out and puts them on the nearest table. He thinks the women may be looking over and so he takes his time, looking to see if there is a spot near Rose. There is, straight across from her. As they approach the table, Jerry puts his arm around Frank and says, "Ladies, I'd like to introduce my father."

"Get outta here," says Frank, pulling away, and the ladies laugh.

Jerry was the comic in their act of comedian and straight man, but Frank could have killed Jerry just now. He looks to Rose. She's smiling. No damage done.

"Great music, Frank," says Winnie, and the others agree. Winnie is flagged by her husband, Jim, who never leaves her side. "You know, it was that very song that we used to dance to at Parlor night?" she says to Jim.

"No, it wasn't," says Jim. "It was Summer, Summer. That was our song."

"Was it?" says Winnie. "I don't remember."

"Ahh," says Jim, waving a hand.

"Hey, Frank, did you see that Charlie O'Neill died?" says Winnie.

"Charlie?" says Frank, taking a moment to remember who Charlie O'Neill was.

Jerry pipes in, "They say that more World War II veterans die each day now than they did during the war." He looks proud of himself for the knowledge, and that time was tougher than the Germans and the Japs had been.

"Can't run from time," says Winnie. That brings a few nods.

The conversation carries on that way for a while. Frank is quiet and he knows the longer he goes, the harder it will be to say something. "It was 1942," interjects Frank.

"What was?" says Jerry.

"This song. The year was 1942. Do you remember, Jer? We took a cargo plane back from France and this was playing in the terminal in New York when we landed."

Jerry looks puzzled. "I think so," he says.

"I just thought it might be fun," says Frank. "Bringing in the old phonograph. You like the song, Rose?"

"I do," says Rose.

"Bringing in the back way, bringing in the front way," sings Winnie, and Ray jumps in, right along beside her.

But Jerry interrupts. "Ope, shhh everybody… Ladler approaching." That brings a few laughs. Old Ry has just emerged from the kitchen. Ry and Mary—and Hattie until she died—worked in the kitchen as ladlers. In the social strata, ladlers were one step up from hungry mouth and one step down from server. It was a job for the infirm; they didn't have to move.

"Hey, Ry, how goes it?" says Jerry.

"Fine," says Ry, giving a sideways glance. He's dressed in an old suit and his mouth hangs open slightly. He sits down with an oomph.

They go back to their conversation. Frank looks over at Rose every so often and manages to get in a word now and then. So close to her now, he's losing his nerve for later. He wonders if he'll be able to ask her, and what she'll say. She's not even Catholic. But then she says to him, "So, Frank, where does the King of the Tables have me working today?"

Frank is elated, and looks at his pad as if he didn't already know and says, "He's got you on two, Rose. And he's got me on one." He smiles and winks.

"That King," she says.

Everyone else is engaged in conversation and Frank doesn't think he can wait. "Say, Rose?"

"Yep?"

But Father Mike appears at the basement steps, and Jerry says, "Speaking of Fathers."

"Bread's here!" calls Father Mike to the back, and Jerry taps Frank on the arm. "Bread's here," he says.

They get up and head out front together, where

Father Mike is waiting with the back of the church truck filled up.

***

It's crisp outside, and Frank wishes he'd put on his coat. The line is beginning to grow, and he glances over to see if the drunk who'd insulted him last week is there. No sign of him just yet. As they approach the truck, Father Mike says, "Hey, boys. What's for lunch?"

"Lasagna," says Jerry.

"Lasagna, lasagna," replies Father Mike, and Frank just smiles and heads for the bread. Frank never knows what to say around Father, who is a young priest and one who rarely wears his Roman collar; and all of a sudden on Sunday you greet your neighbor before mass begins, and hold hands during the Our Father, and for some reason there is no bell ringing at consecration time.

Jerry grabs a few bags stuffed with day-old bread and heads inside. When Frank goes to reach for some himself, Father Mike says, "Frank, I've been meaning to talk to you about something."

Though much had changed about Frank—his sinew now stretched past its tension, his hair just a rectangular silver strip at the back of his head—his eyes have maintained their savage blue, and he looks at Father Mike through them now, for what this might be about.

"Frank, I saw what was happening last week during the meal."

"Rose?" says Frank.

"Excuse me?" replies Father Mike.

Frank shuts up.

Father Mike continues, "That man. The way he said something to you."

"Oh, that," says Frank. "It's not a big deal."

"Well, maybe not, Frank." Father Mike brushes his sweater with his hand, picking away at a stray lint ball. "But there have been a few complaints lately, and not just by the clients."

"What's that?" says Frank.

"It's just that we're in a rush down there at meal time. We serve fifty more meals a day now than we did this time last year. We need those meals out and to the table, not just so the clients can get their meals quickly, but so they can leave and open their seat for the people waiting." He sighs and looks Frank in the eye. "And that man, he's unstable, Frank. Think about the liability we'd have if something were to happen to you."

Frank feels the heat going to his face. His big hands come together, squeeze tightly.

"So we'd like you on ladling duty now, as opposed to working the tables. We'll start with that today."

"No, no, Father. I don't think that's a good idea."

Father Mike puts his hand on Frank's big shoulder. "I thought you might say so, Frank. But it's all God's work."

Frank thinks of Rose. "No, Father, you don't understand."

"I'm going to take your table today, Frank. Until we get someone else to fill it."

Frank is nearly speechless; he tries to keep the conversation going any way he can. "I'd like to play the music through lunch if I could."

Father Mike smiles. "I don't know if that would be appropriate, Frank. Maybe we can discuss it at the meeting next week."

***

Back inside, Frank floats ambiguously between the table he'd assigned himself to cover and the kitchen, where the real boss had put him. The last half hour had been a blur of potential options. He'd disappeared for a while, wandering back to the supply room. Looking into a big box of pasta, he'd yelled, "You're like a Goddamn Protestant minister!" He'd opened and closed his fists. "I was a Marine!"

His anger had brought him back out into the hall, but he was lost once he saw everybody going about their business.

Jerry approaches him now and says, "You don't look so good, Frank. What was that about with Father?"

"Oh," says Frank. "Just a," he stops, clenches his jaw. "That goddamn bum."

"Was it about that creep from last week?"

Frank looks up from the floor and into Jerry's eyes. "No... nope."

"Okay, Frankie, whatever you say." Jerry looks at the clock. It is just a few minutes before the doors will open. "Come on, they're just about ready to beat down the doors." He turns and goes to the serving station where the servers are gathering their trays. Frank looks to Rose, so carefree, banging the tray against her leg like a schoolgirl. He considers up and leaving. But where would Mondays be spent?

Instead of following Jerry, Frank goes to the back entrance to the kitchen. Inside, he takes Hattie's old spot between Ry and Joan. They don't say anything about his being there, as if it is just as natural as could be. "Frank, you're on fruit cup," says old Ry, and he hands Frank a ladle.

***

In the tray in front of him is an assortment of cherries, pears, tangerines, and grapes. He stares into it and feels himself shriveling. His eyes move to the hand that holds the ladle. It looks like someone else's.

Out of the corner of his eye, he sees the servers lined up at the entrance to the kitchen. He stares straight ahead. But that will only make it worse so he forces himself to look over. There's Winnie, Jim, Jerry. Thank God, no Rose. He smiles. "Hey, ho," he says. "Get your fruit cup." He laughs foolishly.

The doors to the outside open and the sound of feet rushing down the stairs fills the kitchen, trampling his will. He knows there won't be tea. But where did it go? Out with the years. This wasn't how he'd lived his life. It didn't mean he had to take it. The servers move through the line. There's a glimpse of Rose's red blouse. And Father Mike.

And all of a sudden, it's 1942 again. Frank jumps out from behind the serving table and rushes out into the hall. A few servers yell for him to stop. "He's going for him!" yells Jerry. But before anyone can get to him, Frank's got old Glenn and his boys pump-pumping at full blast, the hall is nearly shaking with the sound … At last my love has come along, my lonely days are over, and life is like a song, the skies above are…

"Frankie!" calls Jerry.

But Frank is gone, smiling like a child as he disappears up the stairs and out into the blue sky sunshine.

Herbert Wenkel Was Not

Your Average Man

All right. Herbert Wenkel Was Not Your Average Man. Even though, yes, he did live in the middling suburbs of Boston in a neighborhood of gussied-up split-levels and capes. And even though yes he was a mid-level manager in Compliance at Berkley Financial downtown. And even though, yes, outwardly, things like his size and stature and looks and car and education were unremarkable.

But it was Herbert's obsession with a New World Order that placed him at Feng's 8 Miles of Used Books just outside of Harvard Square every Saturday afternoon, standing in his Average Man uniform—boat shoes, Dockers, an old striped shirt—reading in the musty old stacks, dreaming of spades and hoes and seeds sinking into the lovely dark earth. Chesterton, Belloc. The Third Way. There, and not at home, so he could feel a little bit closer to them and to that, at least through the handiwork of the craftsmen from a different age, the soft cloth on all those fading spines, the smell of faded knowledge. He knew his thoughts were simple compared to theirs, but just like them he looked around and lamented… modernity… and he liked to say that he would have been better suited for medieval times—how much better would life be if you lived that much closer to death?—and it was no one thing in particular—just everything—on that particular Saturday when Herbert went home and convinced his wife Jilly that they should do in practice what those men could only write about.

She wasn't a pushover, but she was pliable, and she agreed, because to her, Herbert was quite extraordinary, and definitely not your average man; but also because standing all day long in retail was harder than it looked, and because her suburban idyll had long since faded gray, and because why the heck not when all she'd be leaving behind was what was right there? And so she said, "Yes, I'm ready for anything."

So Herbert and Jilly and their two young boys fled to northern Maine. They bought a small, crumbling dairy farm and apologized to the neighbors for being from Massachusetts and for knowing nothing—absolutely nothing—about dairy farming; and while they did know nothing about dairy farming if they could just figure out how to work within this here system they could make that type of living that they'd hoped to all along. But it took too long to see that there was a reason the people they'd bought from had sold. And while they couldn't afford to fix the broken down everything, Herbert pulled Jilly aside and said this wasn't how you were supposed to do it anyway. "Subsistence farming! Let's go off the grid!"

But Jilly just looked at him. *It gets worse than this?*

Herbert had always been decidedly mediocre when it came to reading his wife. He pressed on. "You remember what I told you? It's all about a different way, a third way, when you're beholden to none…."

Jilly was stone-faced. *Did he see what was here around him? This poverty of scratched-together existence?*

"What you do is, you sell as little as possible, you grow for yourself, and your whole life is a testament to…"

And then she was nearly frothed. "No! We're too normal, too average, we can't go shitting in an outhouse and have our kids running around home-schooled. We can't do that. We couldn't even do THIS!"

Herbert stepped back.

But Jilly wasn't done. "If you want to be closer to God do it on your own time! Do social work, downsize your priorities, but partake of the fruits of modernity. And let's get that 401(k) back to where it should be!"

On their ride back down the Maine Turnpike, Herbert tried to tell himself that while he had glimpsed a little bit of God in those northern Maine mornings—in the steaming potato fields, in the sun rising over the low-rolling mountains, in the feel of the hoe he'd clumsily scratched the ground with—back in that middling suburb he'd come from he'd also recognized God in places, just over a different, uglier landscape. At the same time, he knew he wanted something she didn't. Total devotion wasn't possible in that there first capitalistic system, at least not when you've got kids; if he was all alone he could have walked around ragged—or could he? Jilly would say that's not what He wanted, but Herbert wanted God to answer for him.

He waited. And in the meantime they bought a gussied-up split-level, this time in a different middling suburb and just down the street from a whole new nation of colossal great-roomed dwellings that had seemed to just pop up overnight. Jilly went back to retail, and Herbert fell back into Compliance. And things were mostly back to normal. Except this time on Saturdays, instead of at Feng's 8 Miles of Used Books, you could find Herbert at home in his meager back yard, fumbling through his garden, squeezing dirt and waiting for a bit of that certain something he may never know.

Extrusion

1.

It was just the snarling matter of a man, waiting. Standing in his parlor, taking advantage of the sun on the east side of his street, a street that held the glorious urban polyphony of up and down, in and out, coming and going. Of all of those on this street, Bent felt most up, most in, and that that had its dangers. Rage, anger, hate. Regret.

Here and now it was the widow's turn to give and to receive. She and the thing she called Buff were standing not five feet away on the other side of the glass; she with the obvious posture of someone about to simply leave the extrusion as if it wasn't what it was, and as if Bent was invisible—and to her he was, actually—the August sun repelling any possibility for seeing in. Not that she even cared to look.

This wasn't the Balkans where neighbors turned murderous overnight, but Portland, Maine, where it was the case, as with any other place humans lived, that at a moment's notice you could circle in and find what was easiest to despise about just about anyone. Bent knew her. And he knew her type. Of the three main kinds on this block, she belonged to the original—those living enclosed by tin or vinyl clapboarding on the outside and faux wood-paneling in. Defiant beside gentrified brick and stained glass, and living knowingly, gleefully, among a litany waiting for her death.

Deed done. There she went. Bent sucked on her first step away like a strychnine pop.

White trash! And the mange coming off that creature! Boy, don't they look alike!

It was noon. It was Sunday. And it was all Bent could do to keep himself from opening the window and screaming for the whole world to hear: *Pick it up!*

2.

The paradox. The way something so dirty—the ultimate in physically dirty—could be so cleansing. Not just in the sense that it could be jettisoned, expunged, purged—extruded; but that it could be so grounding. God's reminder? God's joke? And now we are talking human, not canine. The subject of jokes, something to hide, to flush, to cover with spray. The great equalizer! Truck drivers; heiresses. The varieties of shape and composition and size. But why did it have to be what it was? All the hues of the dirtiest rainbow you would ever see. And the nuances, like snowflakes or fingerprints— no two exactly alike.

A certain subsection sees the whole thing clinically; the body sucks out and incorporates, and that's just what happens to be left. Well why couldn't what's left be a tin can, or a perfectly formed square of something that was nice to look at, place on a mantle, or something fun to play with?

But cleansing for him. The widow and the others—the cowards who came and left under the cover of darkness, the hypocrites who bagged only when someone else was about—they provided for him this necessary task, this debasement, this penance, and for that he felt the tiniest bit of gratitude.

"Be right back," to his wife and children, playing melodiously in the next room.

Bag in hand, into the sun. The great and glorious sun. Down the stairs and to the curb. Head hung, as if going to the gallows. Bending and kneeling and feeling the heat at the back of his neck. Hand in bag. The magic of fingers, a palm. Messier than most. A hair. A little piece of something red. Grab and squeeze. <u>Dear Lord, please forgive me… I pick this shit…</u>

It helped him. And that was all.

Service

So here it is: It was Terry Mulvaney's lifelong desire to live the Christian ideal of absolute subordination and obedience, and so he got a job at The Home Depot in South Portland.

He was thirty-three now, and had lived enough of life to know that true callings rarely came at the pointed end of a thunderbolt. It might help you to know that Terry was a lawyer. He hadn't gone to a great law school, but he had passed the Maine bar and went to work for a small law firm in Portland comprised of four lawyers who also hadn't gone to great law schools, but who had banded together because the big firms didn't hire lawyers like them. And those big firms didn't do the type of work that lawyers like them were willing to do. So Terry did house closings and represented clients with motor vehicle violations. He wrote wills. He modified boiler-plate personal injury claims and sent them off to insurance companies, and oftentimes checks would just arrive back in the mail. And then he couldn't do that any more.

All the while he had been looking around, knowing that whatever he would do needed to be done in the context of this American life. He was just a man, and though he thought the American system was rotten, odious, he also thought what the hell was he going to do, change the country, change the world, make everyone live in some type of loving communal system?

The closest thing to a lightning bolt came when he walked into The Home Depot and a sign, handwritten in black magic marker, greeted him:

Our Goal Is To Provide Unsurpassed Customer Service. If You're Not Satisfied, Then We Haven't Done Our Job!

Terry looked around and wondered, But what was customer service? Not the trite catch-phrase that had become the favored buzzword of American business, but the real, true, devoted, honest-to-goodness customer service that could only, only be provided by loving your neighbor with all your might?

So he applied and was accepted and he donned his orange smock and covered it in buttons and wrote right on it in black magic marker: Hi, I'm Terry! He looked customers in the eye. He never pretended he didn't see someone who was obviously looking for assistance. He worked the cash register if they were understaffed. He volunteered for bathroom duty and never shied away from the human stink left behind. He even printed his name in clear block letters on the "This Bathroom was Last Cleaned By:" list, though he was only required to give initials. And when his boss, a high school educated twenty-five-year-old who had never made it above plumber's apprentice, said, "Terry could you come here for a minute?" Terry always dropped everything and went right away.

After having heard all this you might say, "Big deal! That's a good paying job! Plenty of people would want to work at The Home Depot; he's getting stock options, for the love of God! You're just a goddamn snob! Why shouldn't he want to provide good customer service? That's what he's getting paid for!" And then you might shake your head and say, "It's all very dramatic."

And Terry would say, "That's the truth." He wouldn't disagree at all. He would just welcome you to The Home Depot and make sure your every need was attended to.

poplars outside her windows, bringing the baker's yellow of the kitchen walls into full bloom. She would sit and sip her coffee and watch the light's progression through the kitchen, down the tea-green hallway, and on into the sitting room, oriental jade.

Their house was a twelve-room Victorian in the West End, a section of the city that could have been a lot of different places if you were dropped right down inside it: Westmount just outside Montreal, Beacon Hill in Boston, Park Slope, Brooklyn—all places she and David had lived together. Portland was some of the things those places were, but more, and just enough less—it was why they'd moved there to start a family. They had talked endlessly about the type of house they wanted, and they got it. It was a dream—the brocaded entry, the mahogany staircase, the sculpted ceilings. She and David decorated with passion. They picked their colors carefully, staying within the period scheme outside, a classic flat olive, accented with coriander and gray, while inside was their opportunity for expression, each room a creation, mauve and eggplant and pale-fire red. And when they were done they breathed in deeply. It was the living palate they had always hoped to be consumed by.

But then through Elsie's pregnancy things started to bleach. David asked what was wrong and Elsie just shrugged. Sometimes at night she would walk through the house while David slept, attempting to evoke that first feeling she had had when deciding on the clean lines of the Farmer's Table from the Mission Valley catalogue, or that first excitement she had had upon discovering the pleasing folds and tawny sheen of the mustard curtains that had once hung in the display room at Rue Charlemagne. Sometimes it worked, if only until morning.

And then Charlie came. Under the sterile, gleaming lights of the hospital room, they could hardly believe their eyes. The word for what he was popped into Elsie's head, but she popped it right back out. He's just very white, she told herself, extraordinarily so. Before he was born she had thought of the reasons she would tell him he was special—your mommy and daddy love you, Charlie; you're kind, and you're brilliant, and God loves you, too—but she had never considered having to tell him he was also special because of his condition. It was occulocutaneous.

Of course, she had a mother's love, but at first there he was, a little suckling bandit, an alien on her breast, pinkish eyes closed to keep out the light. When they brought him home, they smiled like they should have, but everything was out of place.

There was a string of doctors and consultations. The marriage counselor told them it was a condition that affected not only Charlie, but her, and David, too. Knowing very well what he meant, Elsie said anyway, "Well, you're right about that. We're both carriers or Charlie couldn't have it. We just have the recessive genes." She saw David squirm, as if to deny it. The counselor folded his hands and said, "Maybe you had sensed it in each other and that's what drew you two together." But Elsie looked at David as if to say, Is that what I saw in you, latent albinism?

Time went on and they adjusted accordingly. That wasn't all that hard to do; Charlie was a blessed little thing, crawling, and then running through the rooms of their house, a little beacon. So many times, the three of them together, enveloped by the peach or the cream or the Mariner's blue, it was glorious. And outside, too. But there would always be some little thing, like David bundling Charlie up for a walk, even on the warmest of days, or she herself, with the straight-ahead gaze she'd perfected for Story Hour at the library and her glazed mind to match. It wasn't shame; you could just get tired of all those eyes.

Elsie was pregnant again now, but she wasn't looking for anything particular in the sun that morning as she sat in the kitchen, and she wasn't looking to see what it did to the colors of her house. It was all just pigmentation. Now, she just liked to concentrate on the facts—that David would be down soon, still looking so much like the man that, even as a little girl, she knew she would marry; and that soon after that Charlie would be up, white and extraordinary, but hard, sometimes, to look in the eye; and what it was was a rainbow of things, that looking at him reminded her of what she and David were, which was obvious, or translucent, or just too caring, wanting a normal life for their son and to keep all those eyes away, but most of all, it was that they had the whiteness, too. And she tried to remind herself of that every day.

Suit Coat

The green trees of Pont-Sous had been enough to choke on. But that hadn't stopped John Porfous and his best friend Lyle from flaring their pants at the bottoms and letting them sag off their rear ends, as if the forest was the projects and the wildlife all around them the city's danger. Trees were Pont-Sous. But now Pont-Sous was a dying little town way up in Maine's north and west, on the border with Quebec. John didn't care so much about the opportunity that had been there for Porfouses for generations but had now run out because of foreign competition and inefficient mills and because clearcutting had left most areas ravaged. He had never wanted to be a timber man anyway.

So while Lyle talked about living in Portland or maybe even Boston, it was John who pecked away at the classifieds in the state-wide Sunday paper. That went on for a while until finally it was John's former shop teacher at the high school, Mr. Reed, who managed to secure a job for him. He knew someone and it had happened so quickly.

At first, John wasn't even sure what to do. He had been as far as Bangor just once in his entire life and never south of that. When he packed up his truck and headed east on 402 past St. Therese and on into Steubenville and beyond—a route he had only traveled a dozen or so times in his life—there was some foreign energy running through him that was equal parts good fortune mixed with anxiety and the guilt of leaving his parents behind. His father had actually hugged him.

He found himself a spot in a motel thirty miles outside of Portland in a sparse little town that reminded him of home. He drove his truck back and forth to his job on Portland's waterfront as a welder, collecting paychecks and skipping one meal a day until he could afford a place of his own. Things had gone smoothly, mostly, but what it had really been was six weeks of firsts: first time not sleeping in the bed he had grown up in; first time going to a job where his father wasn't the boss; first time seeing a building that was higher than three stories tall; first time seeing a black face in person. And now, just yesterday, first time in his own apartment.

He had called about it from a payphone. The voice of an old lady had said to meet her there, 65 Prince Street on Munjoy Hill. John was a full hour early, sitting in his truck and just staring up at the house, which was the shape of a rectangular box. It was four floors and vinyl-sided and was attached to a building just like it by a dark balcony that served as both respite and fire escape. It stood in a row of houses that were more or less the same, and as he stared on up at it, he realized he had absolutely no idea what to expect inside.

When an old lady appeared in a housedress outside the front door John wasn't sure it was her but he took a chance and it was. He followed her up the stairs, staring at the backs of her prickly calves, and soon they were at an apartment door, number 402.

They entered and she led him through the three rooms, talking only in clipped directives: "Place is mostly furnished, you break anything you pay for it;" "Trash is on Wednesday, you put it out yourself not before seven the night before;" "Hot water's good for only a minute or two, so there's no sense lingering in the shower."

When they got to the last room, the kitchen, the old lady stopped to look at him, whether it was to gauge his interest or what he didn't know, but under her eyes he felt as if he should perform, and so as his heart pushed precious blood up to his temples he went to the room's only window and looked out it. "That's common space out back," she said. "You share it with the rest of the building. You gonna take it?"

All John could do was nod. He signed something and gave her the rent in cash—and he hardly noticed her after that.

***

Someone standing outside looking in might have thought there was a madman in there, the way John walked back and forth from room to room as if one might disappear if he didn't check on it. It was the little thoughts popping into his head that propelled him: ...a microwave, and the little stove, just two burners but I bet that cooks good! A sturdy table with four chairs. Why is it kitty-corner, though? Better over there by that window, but maybe I shouldn't move it just now… He'd stop for a while and contemplate how this thing or that could be used, even if it was just the sitting room chair. Then he'd continue on, overcome by the desire to talk, but keeping it to himself, but still making the point that, Wasn't it nice the way the light shined in on the bedroom at that time of day? And those were good, wide, pine floor boards. Not unlike what used to be cut up there in Pont-Sous. Pont-Sous. He pushed that away.

It went on that way for quite some time; and it was only later that he noticed the closet at the end of the hall. He had mistaken it for a wall because the door was nearly painted shut and there was no handle.

He scraped at it a bit and then opened the door slowly to savor this last discovery. There inside, on a hanger, was a suit coat. He studied it for a moment as if to make sure it was what it was. It would have been no stranger had a monkey been hanging there upside down. He had never had a suit coat before. It was blue, and he lifted one of the sleeves. The line of three shiny brass buttons leading up from the cuff tinkled together when he let the sleeve drop. He stepped back.

Dead Man Walking

So in crisp red and khaki, standing in Target's Homewares was Lazarus—Sudanese, Azande, just three months removed from two years hiding in Yemen, his deep black skin having made him a target himself, Christian refugee muck—and the sun would soon be rising over the parking lot. How would he get home?

It was the first crack in the last three months that had played like a symphony, an orchestration of lifting, hoisting, stacking; out from the darkness of his small room in downtown Portland and into Nelson's rusting, donated minivan for the too-quick ride through the bright and colorful order of all those shops and restaurants, Bug-a-boo… Dick's… Pizzeria… But now Nelson had gone

Andrew McNabb

away to live with cousins recently arrived in a place called Michigan.

"Mo da ka wa mo gbata kura gene," Nelson had said. You'll have to find some other way.

So Lazarus took the bus for the first time last night. It was just him and the driver on the slow-droning bus, and outside his window was an even different world. Bug-a-boo…

Creek…

Dick's…

Sporting Goods…

Pizzeria…

Uno.

That had been the last bus available, but he was still two hours early. He'd sat in the luncheonette with a hot dog in front of him, waiting for his overnight shift to begin at nine, wondering what he would do in the morning, when instead of two hours, he'd have to wait for three.

At the two a.m. lunch break, while sitting in the luncheonette drinking Pepsi and eating cold lamb stew, he had had an idea: Maybe he could crawl into the circle of two that was Jimmy and Kevin; they were

94

always laughing, and they had a name for him—what was it? DMW? "What up, DMW?"—and maybe he could ask them for a ride home. But as they sat at the next table giggling over a plate of nachos, Lazarus lost his nerve.

But as had happened many times in these last few years, something popped up to save him. Standing, still, in Housewares, the boxes of blue and white and red spatulas opened and unpacked and waiting to be hung, the sun itself provided an answer. Glinting at first light off the glass of the Babies-R-Us across the way, illuminating the barren access road that he could now see clearly, and down which, he knew, was that great and colorful order and then beyond it, his home. He knew the way. It wasn't very difficult, he told himself. He would, quite simply, walk.

Body by Body Glove

Lydia Carmona was a short, squat acorn among the oak trees. Of the ways in which that could be carried forward, perhaps the most profound was the end result of what she'd chosen to clothe her body with that day. But where she lived couldn't be discounted. If Portland could be broken into a dozen bits, one of them would be a clump of vinyl-sided three-deckers in an area that no one knew what to call, separated from the rest of the city by a curve in the highway, and fortified by a series of businesses housed in plain-faced cinder block buildings. "Tegucigalpa and Portland Made Me," could have been the title of the autobiography of her young life.

But her clothing; Lydia was a fashion major at Portland Arts & Vocational High School, where she had learned that fashion was art. Though her mother had been a seamstress in Mexico and her father a tailor, they would have had a hard time understanding what Mr. Samuellson, the department head, had said to the gathering of fashion majors on Lydia's first day of school: "Good fashion makes a statement. If you were to dig deep into your soul and pull something out, what would it be?" Lydia pictured Our Lady of Guadalupe, but shook that away because, really, who in this day was going to wear a flowing gown of sparkling chartreuse?

Today was Fashion Friday, the day each year when the fashion majors wore their own creations. It was the favorite day of the designers, and also the favorite day of the future plumbers and electricians and carpenters of America, who would laugh and point at what came down the hallways.

And because these were the modern times, Lydia had her own message. This thing she was wearing, she was calling it a Body Glove. All it was was two tubular swatches of stretchable fabric that could be held in the palm of your hand.

She'd put it on in her room and exploding back at her from the mirror was not a pattern or a fashion or a style, but curves and rolls and a broad, deep belly button. Big breasts flipped out to the sides like overripe bananas. Wide, wide hips. And centering it all, a little love trail heading down to that spot right there, where life itself was fashioned from.

Today. Today would be a good day. They'd notice who she was. And she didn't care what they'd say.

Rapture

These are quarky streets, she tells me. When she tells me this, the wet is practically dripping from her teeth. The teeth in her mouth are downright brown. I can only imagine how they got to be that way. She is, maybe, forty. How many meals from the time she was a child went unbrushed? How must it feel to run your tongue along your teeth and feel a persistent grit? She is almost inhuman. I can not relate. My teeth have been washed and picked clean.

I am here to kiss her mouth. Not a kiss of passion but a kiss of function, though passion shall be a part of it, because in that passion there will be a message of understanding, of equality. I am here to kiss her mouth, to rub her teeth free of their pearly little bumps with my tongue. I will brush for her. I will be her brush. But I can not restore her teeth to white. Only God can do that!

If you are me, you have come here from a sturdy place. This place is anything but. Oh, but it is in its own way! It is sturdy because it is ascendant. Though there is certainly evil here, too. But this is baseness. And because of that it is an absolutely thrilling and monumental spot. We are just down—and when I say down, I mean down in a physical sense, because this city here has been built on a hill making it look higher than it actually is—but we are just down, three blocks from the city center. Three rolling, tumbling blocks. They are long blocks. But they are just three. And yet the nature and shape of nearly everything—buildings, streets and, especially, people—is so very different here than just three blocks higher.

This place is a gaggle of exotic parts, none more so than those of this woman. This woman. I have sought her out. I have seen her. I see her.

Quarky, she says again. Brown. *Quarky!* Where would she come up with such a word, such a description? The beauty and surprise of pure human potential! And she has taken to me the way I have taken to her. What compassion! She is trying to help me. I am new here. She sees that. I stare at the teeth in her mouth. I will tongue them clean. Oh, if my wife and children only knew I was here!

I will tell them, but for now I am here where the sun is low in the beautiful winter sky, obscured by one long cloud, a mass of gray, providing pure monochrome comfort. It is just cold enough to be jumpy, a cold that intensifies a limb's movements and, thankfully, a cold in which a body can be immersed for hours without danger, and that is important here, because these are outdoor wanderers, their skin hardened, stretched tightly over their bodies.

Huh, I reply.

Her nipples shoot out and flip down like light switches turned off. I have seen her breasts before. Or one breast, deflated and dirty. It was months ago, a Saturday, that first exuberant Maine spring day when it was certain the cold had gone for good. She was on her back on a patch of grass over at the public park a few blocks away. I was with my family in our car at a red light. A man was lying beside her. There was a party going on. Three men and two women under a big lush tree. All of a sudden, a spectacular kiss, disorganized and wild, tongues missing mouths, licking faces. The party went on around them. My wife and children weren't watching, they were singing. In the scrum, her shirt lifted up, a breast flapped out and to the side. A flat and dirty vessel. She stopped and they looked at it. They laughed. She covered up and they kissed again and I was the one, fully clothed and tight inside my own skin, who felt inhuman. The light turned green.

I am not undercover now. And I am not here for long. I have seen her in the city center. She has smiled at me so many times before, one time coming when I was with a colleague; "Indian corn teeth," he said, and we laughed. But I didn't tell him that I had seen her breast. Lovely, splayed. It is my secret. And hers, though she doesn't know it. I might tell her. She doesn't seem to recognize me.

It is so late in the day, an ordinary Tuesday at the onset of winter. What the hell am I supposed to do about everything? I have flipped off most of me and am here just as I am. All I want to do is walk. Walk here, walk for miles, just keeping on walking and coming back here, in the modest shadow of medium-sized buildings in this medium-sized city where, true to life, some things are large and some things are small.

And this woman, this beautiful woman. Hair tangled like an aphid's nest. *Quarky.* I want to leave here and go to the park with her. I want to lie on a blanket on the ground under a rich and fertile tree. I want to put my tongue in her mouth and clean her teeth of their ferment, and to lift, gently, that breast sagging from life. Rapture.

Precious Blood

There is a line of tall green pine trees at the back of the lot of the Monastery of the Precious Blood on State Street. In the context of the plot and its components—building, driveway, landscape—these trees are not fence and not ornamentation, but a green canvas of contrast for those who are there to look at the statue of Christ head-on.

Rae-Rae Furcal is not one of those. He is a monkey, an ape. He has climbed the tallest tree and sits high up so he is obscured from the world, and so that he can study the statue from behind. The white marble man has parted hair. God, Himself, with parted hair. In the village square in Ticun, in Oaxaca, where he is from, there is a painted wooden statue of Our Lady of Guadalupe with eyes dripping and so real that no one dares look directly into them. This Jesus is simply frozen.

What he thinks of now is how cold it is here. How he is short. Those twenty-three steps up to the third floor apartment on Washington Avenue that he shares with five other men. The smell of American dirt inside.

As the bodies pass by on the sidewalk in front of the monastery, he asks the back of Jesus's head why he was led by the Holy Spirit over the border and then all the way up to this city, Portland, in this state called Maine.

After a while, an answer comes in the brightness of the sky before his eyes, in the ridges of the bark in his hands, in the sound of the cars whizzing smoothly by. And now, with his eyes closed, in the feel of the blood coursing thickly through his veins.

Beep.

A Small City

Tim Gaddis was no architect. What he was was an investment specialist (and his own therapist). When he thought about it, which was often, and right now, he thought about how he could talk stocks. CEO movements, the Fed, the economy, interest rates, even LIBOR, FTSE, the DAX. He'd been at this long enough, eighteen years, to talk with conviction because he understood most of what he was saying—at least as much as anyone really understood or knew what they were saying; there wouldn't be financial modeling and stochastic processes and quant jocks and differing opinions on every stock out there and where the economy was going if it was purely subjective matter—but that wasn't the deal right now.

The deal right now was how he felt when he walked into and out of his office at Sixty-Six Center in downtown Portland, Maine. He and Janessa and their two young boys had moved to Portland from northern New Jersey three months prior for the quality of life. You made less, but it didn't take as much. He had transferred and now he was in Meridian Financial's local investor center, which comprised the bottom floor of that squat six-story building where the brick and glass were separated by a series of poured cement columns. The building was part of a cluster, all similarly-sized—a small-city financial center—filled, mostly, with the corporate outposts of major financial companies.

But while poured cement columns spread six feet apart and going from base to roof in some type of reference to the Greeks was supposed to, perhaps, elongate the building's feel, evoke a sense of grandeur, all it seemed to do was puff out a meager chest. Some days it felt like everything about his new location was askew, especially the inside of the building where—although the furniture, literature, artwork, and carpeting were standardized across all branches, and if you squinted hard enough you could have been in the midtown Manhattan branch he'd come from—the fact remained that there was only one burgundy-hued greeter's counter. In midtown there were twenty-two and that pretty much said it all.

But Jesus Christ, he thought, that wasn't the way you were supposed to think of it. Anybody could talk stocks. It wasn't like he had been downsized, too. No, this was what he was, what he needed to be. A small jewel. A place that other people wanted to come to, to live.

He was, a small city.

Tootsie

Tootsie Wilcox was wondering just when she had become a mother. Not a *mother* mother, but <u>someone's</u> mother; when had that little sag dropped down and moved in for good, when had short hair become preferable for its ease; when had she become completely—even blissfully—unaware of contemporary music in favor of classical and NPR?

Well, tonight would be different. She would have sex with Rob. It was Monday, and Saturdays had been their routine. While Hannah took her afternoon nap, Tootsie put on the negligee from their wedding night. Had it really been that small?

That night at the dinner table Rob farted and she

ignored it. She loved him, and you overlooked those things, bodily functions. And then while they were putting Hannah to sleep he farted again. That time he laughed. But she loved him. Whenever it was time to make love, she was still attracted to him, his still-strong pectorals, his weight on top of her. While she finished up the dishes right before bed, she realized something— there seemed to be a moratorium on flatulence on Saturdays.

When she walked into the bedroom, Rob was already in bed reading. She took off her clothes and didn't trade in the negligee for pajamas. He didn't seem to notice. What would her next move be? When she lifted the covers, the faint scent of flatulence wafted up from under the covers.

Rob looked up and smiled. "I love you, honey," he said.

She hopped into bed. "I love you, too."

They kissed and she reached for her book, a romance. She settled in for the night.

moments to "All Things Considered," heart pulsing, awaiting the introduction, when she'd listen for the slightest hint of what was to come from Robert Siegel, Mee-chelle Norris. Was that a melancholic inflection, a dolorous note? Would today's tragedy be rich enough?

Misfortune hadn't been rated on a scale of one to ten, but death and/or dismemberment of children rated high on the feeling factor. Soldiers, too. That meant not just lives cut short, but widows and fatherless children. Exhale. Tragic. But please no leads from south Asia. There it would have to be total death and destruction, not just a train collision killing ten. And what if the headline was just political? That was too slow a death when what was needed was a junkie's fix. In that case, off went the Bose in the marbled-out kitchen and out to make her own headlines. The Ronald McDonald house wasn't far away. Stand across the street and watch. Take off that cap, young man, let's see that head bald from chemo! What are you feeling, mother? And if that wasn't enough, there were always the archives at the library: 9/11 building jumpers, Holocaust trains, body counts in Rwanda.

But forget all that—there it was!—everything she needed right before her. Mother Mary, pray for us! Mary

Magdalene, pray for us! You were a whore, and so was I! And now she didn't need that daily dose of "All Things Considered."

The tragedy? That it was blank outside her window. Nothing. Just a bridge over Casco Bay, connecting one beautiful place to another. So there'd be no more, What to do now? No more, Give it all up and join the Peace Corps? No more, Simply pay tithes? Or, think globally, act locally, volunteer at the St. Vincent de Paul Soup Kitchen? *Ha! No more!*

A cool sea-breeze blew through an open window, and Barbara settled in with her afternoon tea. With that too-beautiful view. If only she had the time.

Compartments

There are such things as compartments and the buildings that house them. I'd like to tell you about mine. Here, in my area, at a thousand feet there is rapture. On a cloudless day, mountains to the west, one great explosion above all others, white-capped no matter the season, and green, green trees. To the East, cold ocean and piney islands popping up from the depths, small and secure, a labyrinth, some pre-conceived network. Centering it all was man's brick, red and orange and rimmed with the white of mixed-up sand. In the forefront, on the cusp of blue ocean, uneven structures, big buildings and small. A hill to the north and east where rows of triangular houses and compartment buildings are arranged side-by-side. And on the other side of downtown, where my compartment is, a more varied maze, and where the brick gets redder. Consume the whole, but notice the details: the church spires, the wide avenues, the narrow lanes, the asphalt, the cobblestone, the wood.

Now drop down closer to just above the rooftops. My structure, my compartment building, a rectangular box. No different in principle than a shoebox that becomes a child's toy—insert a grid to break up the space, put one small doll in here and another in there and watch them go. So here it is, two rows of four compartments on three floors, three dimensionally, each compartment housing the essentials for today's life. But let's not go inside just yet; come down further and study the outside of the structure first. Brown brick, not red. And of a varied mold, rougher and more textured. Don't forget that that was some person's idea, <u>Let's use a different type of brick, a different color, how about brown? And let's make it a different texture, too, and let's call this building The Alsop Arms.</u> That's quite a name, a proper name, even though this building was never anything other than what it is, a structure to house the common. Common?

Before we get to that, let's stay with the outside of the structure where the brick is brown and the window frames are painted yellow. Yellow. A very particular shade, dark and thick and hearty enough to stand up to the dominant brown speckled with bits of mica and sediment. Brown and yellow, a not uncommon pairing of colors, but uncommon in the world of brick, so this building stands out, and not just for that reason, but because of its architecture. Functional, utilitarian, rectangular, twelve compartments of equal size and equal amenity. But that didn't mean eighty-seven years ago that you didn't ring the top floor with an artist's sculpted cement. And it didn't mean that the front door would be made of anything other than a dark old-growth oak, carved and fashioned. And it didn't mean that you wouldn't put at the entrance a window of leaded glass, colored deeply red.

There is a sidewalk of cracked red brick out front. A contrast. Red brick and brown brick. There is red brick everywhere in this city. Yet this structure has been made of brown brick and rimmed with yellow. Trees have grown up outside it, splitting the red brick sidewalk. Trees tall and tough and shading the structure so that it is damp and so that the wooden window sills show rot. But those are on the outside, not the inside. Sills on a compartment building can rot outside until the rot begins to affect the inside, and then it will be addressed, and when replaced, standing in for something sculpted and crafted will be something standard, pressed in to action to stop the flow of rain or air or to hold up the box that cools the compartment. Functional, utilitarian, but only, of course, in a modern sense.

Now take a look around, but not for too long. This is a brown brick building rimmed with yellow, and right beside it on one side is a structure made entirely of wood. It is painted aubergine and highlighted with army green and khaki. There is one doorbell and one mailbox and so this structure is prim. Ornamental woodwork drips from the gutters like beautiful rain. On my structure's other side is a gabled and intricate structure of red brick. A virtual mansion. Right here. Right beside the Alsop Arms. A completely different life, with completely different expectations. And beside that, another compartment building, plainer than mine, just a box, really. But let's leave these structures and all other structures within eyeshot because they have their own stories and to look at them too closely is to spend too much time, and to not study them is to not understand. Just know that they are part of this symmetry of wood and brick, some compartment buildings, some not, all of them together making up this street, this area.

Now, come inside.

That's an intricate door.

These are fading tiles.

Those are mailboxes pushed into the wall, to be opened with tiny keys.

These are good wide stairs, heavily banistered and covered repeatedly with coats of shiny, smooth paint to weather the millions of touches and pulls.

To the second of three floors, and through this heavy door recently inserted for the purpose of a code. Given its placement, it was not intended by the designer of this building. It is newer and plainer, but stronger, and what was surrendered in the form of the shape and the feel of this hallway has been made up in the concern for life, or simply in the realization of what can occur in the event of a mistake inside a structure like this.

That's my door in the middle. There are bumps and noises on either side of me, and above and below. That right there is the compartment of a woman who has walked this earth for eighty-three years. She is just four years younger than this structure. Too many comparisons could be drawn between them, perhaps the most symbolic being her cracked skin always done up with a particularly clownish rouge. Her hair, for the public, is synthetic, and for herself, inside her compartment, short like a military man's. She has lived here forty-one years. In that same compartment. A whole life, so that this hall and that door and those walls can be felt by her mind with the closing of her eyes and the rubbing of her fingers. She is this structure, and if she has an issue it is that she doesn't want them to change her door, bruised from a thousand meaningless kicks, because then her monthly sum will increase. She bases her life on 1956 dollars.

Above me is a couple. Their skin is printed with a rainbow of colors and designs, their bodies, in parts, punctured by silver. They look the other way, shyly, when they see me. They are shockingly quiet. They are the artists of their own structures, in the same way the creators of this brown brick building were. Let's paint our skin this way, they must have said, though in dribs and drabs, in these designs and in these colors! And surely, undoubtedly, whatever is contained inside their compartment blends with the patterns on their skin. But who would have guessed that they would be so hushed?

It's about them and it's about the old woman and it's about the young woman on the other side of me who, of us all, is just a temporary visitor. And that's because of the way her body has been constructed, her backside bumping out just enough to evoke an apple, a peach. Her eyes, almonds. Prim nose and teeth and chin. She doesn't really live here. She is just a visitor. She is young. This structure is temporary shelter. Someone will be along to take her from it and into his own. She goes about living every day as if she knows that, and that it will happen at any moment, the way she comes and goes, swinging that pink bag that holds her things.

There are others, of course. You can go up and down these halls knocking on doors, and answering will be the heads and bodies of humans, the smells coming from behind their doors the cologne of their lives. A mysterious stew, or marijuana, or cheap perfume. We are what we smell like. So what does my compartment smell of? Most of the time I can't tell. For some reason that's because I live there, but every once in a while, upon entering, it comes to me, whatever it is, this concoction, and then it departs just as suddenly. How pleasing or how unpleasant is for me to decide as I keep on mixing.

Now step inside, breathe the air deeply and look up. What do you see? Moldings and plaster and the frosted glass of an exposed light. And down, a floor of man's fabrication, not nature's. Walk about, note the hardware, the places to rest, the structures that hold things, all the colors, all the shapes, their conditions, the plant life, the pictures, the paintings, the things on the floor and in the drawers. Look around. See me, smell me. Listen for my neighbors. Imagine their lives. But it is the outside of this building that says all you need to know. We have all chosen to shelter ourselves beneath this roof.

These are compartments, and this is a compartment building, and as you pull away, depart, ascend, and keep on rising it all becomes clearer, this particular life, this particular structure as part of the network of this street, this area, the semi-ordered maze this side of downtown. Higher and higher, smaller and smaller, clearer and then more distant before it all disappears and an entirely different landscape emerges.

Habeas Corpus

It was funny how a little woman-paunch could make for a brighter than expected lunch. But that's exactly what happened when Michelle (Morris) Dunlap emerged from around the corner outside Natasha's restaurant at Post Office Square in the Old Port to meet her best friend growing up, Dee Dee (Schill) Sainsbury. It had been twelve years since they had seen each other; twelve no-more-momentous years, from twenty-three to thirty-five, when it came to the depreciation of certain physical assets.

Dee Dee's particular depreciation had been steep and fast and could be easily and conveniently blamed on that second child being pulled through the hole they'd cut in her lower abdomen, severing muscle tissue that just didn't want to go back to form. But that wouldn't have been correct, exactly. The cut, the organs lifted and placed on top of her stomach, the baby extraction, the organ reinsertion, and the being sewn back up was a lot to come back from, true, but as early as Dee Dee's teens one could have seen the potential for trouble in the hint of a shimmer at the backs of her thighs and in the hanging looseness of her upper arms. She'd managed to keep herself on the right side of medium by exercising and dieting, and she'd been getting back to that a bit lately, but it just seemed to make her go more sagged; and combine that now with the recent, stark, astonishing discovery that her husband, who had never had issues of his own, who was naturally thin and athletic and pre-disposed to exercise as if it was *actually fun*, while bending down in front of her after a recent morning shower, all of a sudden possessed, between his chest and his genitals, a flabby little flesh hammock as if right out of nowhere. *If it could happen to him…*

But that didn't help Dee Dee in the mirror that morning, paunch in hands, retaining water, bloated and about to get her period and unable to look too far down for fear of the creeping presence of that spider vein that was making its way up the inside of her thigh; and in keeping her eyes away she couldn't help but focus on the hair, creeping itself, out the sides of her underwear and she flashed back to the pool at the golf club they had belonged to when she was a child where all of the mothers (except Mrs. Le Brun, who was smooth and taut despite her age and whom, it was common knowledge, all the daddyies stared at) held bodily court, a menagerie of dropping physiques, and when you're perky and lithe and fourteen you know you'll never look like that. But that's exactly how they looked.

But she couldn't bow out of the lunch now—she was the one who had called for it. Michelle was in town for just a few days. So Dee Dee put on those black slacks, the ones that would serve her best, as slimming as anything besides a corset could possibly be. She pulled and pulled, higher and higher, hoping to make that bubble disappear—but, no, just the opposite. The words were already pursed on her lips: <u>Oh, this damn baby weight, I'm having such a hard time getting it off.</u>

It wasn't until she was actually standing outside Natasha's, sucking herself in, that she even considered what Michelle might look like. She barely had time to ponder it when from around the corner came Michelle, bright-faced and smiling and wearing, perhaps, the ugliest—and thus most beautiful—dress Dee Dee had ever seen. Not cheap, of course—not on Michelle, doctor's daughter, doctor's wife—but just plain ugly and designer plaid but so beautiful in its accentuation of what was most definitely, beyond question, *a category two paunch!* Round and low, ascending up from the pubis or heading down from the belly, it was hard to tell, but it didn't really matter. Pretty, thin, perky Michelle, voted most likely in Dee Dee's mind to be her circle's Mrs. Le Brun, was paunched and primed, and on she came, throwing open her arms, lunging herself into physical human contact. They touched, deepened belly button to deepened belly button like two mouths engaged in a French kiss; and the result was no less profound. Why does wisdom rely so often on the physical, Dee Dee wondered, when that bulge and that sag was a clear and blessed acknowledgement of the obvious, inevitable corporeal descent? The failure to bounce back wasn't a problem, it was just the shape of her body's decay.

The realization was positively religious. Her mind wanted to lead her down that road, but for now she hugged, and hugged hard. It was wonderful seeing her old friend. Their bellies disengaged, and she couldn't wait to get inside. She was famished.

It's What It Feels Like

I know I shouldn't, but sometimes when I look at Clara I wish she had even more meat to her face. She doesn't look like she did in high school when there was no meat there at all, just creamy skin over well-pronounced cheekbones; but love will make you see that fat folds are just that—folds of fat, and despite her having to wear polyester flex clothes, I can't help but see Clara as that skinny high school girl with those cheekbones and tight jeans and a cigarette dangling from her hand.

I'm a thin man and don't let anyone ever tell you that being thin is a blessing. If you're a man, it's better to be on the other side of average, especially here in Timber, Maine where ideal physiques are bulked for chopping wood and for keeping out the cold—not posing for six-pack tummy shots in one of those silly men's magazines. I could eat three plates of spaghetti a day and never gain an ounce, whereas Clara says all she has to do is look at a piece of chocolate cake and she gains a pound right there.

But her fat in my life has been a good thing. It's been the great equalizer. It brought us together. Without it, she'd still be with her ex-husband, Rob, who dumped her a year and a half ago for a high school version of herself. It's like that TV you don't have the money for one day, and you go back the next and it's half-price because there's a crack in the plastic. It's the same TV, but it's cracked, so you can afford it. Well that's Clara, except the crack is fat, and if she was as slim as she used to be I'd just be looking at her in the display window not sleeping beside her every night. It is what it is, and there's no use saying otherwise. I love her, not because of what she was or how she used to look, but because of what she is now, which is a whole slew of those words people come up with when they have to talk about someone they love and aren't allowed to mention looks—like she's witty and compassionate and caring.

So Rob's loss is my gain, and it's one of those things that makes life what it is, a beautiful but confusing experience. I can't understand how people can have these visions in their minds of what they want—of what they think they want—when right in front of them, or even in their very hands, is what's most desirable, if their minds would just let their fingers feel, and if their fingers would just let their minds think. I always tell Clara when she's feeling down about herself that life isn't what it looks like, but what it feels like, and that she feels sublime to me.

It's a shame that that's not always the way people see things and some of those distorted thoughts have been creeping into Clara's mind lately, and she's been losing weight as a result. I don't want to be paranoid, but it seems that started right around the time Rob, and the woman he left her for, Melanie, broke off their engagement. That was two months ago, and since then I've seen the changes in her body, and in her voice, in the way she's been talking to me, or hasn't been. Maybe Clara thinks being back together with Rob would be trading up, I don't know. I want to remind her that before she found out about Rob's breakup she was as calm as could be, the way we'd sit at the kitchen table looking out the can think about is Clara, and how I wish there was even more meat to her face.

***

Timber, Maine is a place time forgot, or so I'm told. I haven't spent much time in other places to know for sure. It's in the middle of the state and not near enough any mountain or lake to make it a place people from out of state want to vacation, and I've always thought that that's a good thing. You may hear folks say on the news and in the papers that Mainers are friendly, that we live in what the state government calls "Vacationland," but if you ask the average Mainer if he likes having to depend on people from Massachusetts and New York driving up on weekends and spending money for his livelihood, most would say no.

Back in school there was this kid, Joey Salvucci, who came here from East Boston for the summers to stay with his grandmother. Joey would arrive on the Fourth of July and leave on Labor Day, having kissed half the girls in town. He'd say at least once every time you were with him how awful it was in Timber, and that he was only there because there was too much shit to get into back home. Rednecks he called us, and shit-shovelers.

He'd tell us what it was like living in the city and made it seem that living here was like living in a place with no sun, no sky, no nothing. It always seemed to me, though, that he had a great time, smoking joints and tubing in the river, and especially with the girls, who thought he was some type of god just because he was from someplace else. I think of him every time someone happens to stop in town with out-of-state plates. Whether they're at the gas station or the diner or the supermarket, they're always looking at you; and I know what they're thinking: So that's what someone who lives in the middle of nowhere looks like.

But the middle of nowhere can be damn good in my opinion, and thankfully, here in Timber we don't rely on the tourist trade very much. North American Pulp and Paper stands on the banks of the Merton River, which flows down from Canada, coke-colored and frothy. The mill employs about half the town in one capacity or another.

Like most mill towns, Timber was once a greater place, with more people and brighter prospects, but we've survived. Life here is what most people would call simple—going to work and living non-working hours whatever way you'd like. People meet at the coffee shop or at one of the three bars or the few restaurants, or they go off hunting or fishing or things like that. There's a movie theatre downtown, and the local high school sports teams are usually pretty good entertainment. Clara and I do things together, mostly play cards and go for walks or out for nice dinners. Her daughter, Lexie, is eight years old, and so that right there takes up a good portion of our free time. It's all been great, until Rob's ass got dumped and he started sniffing around Clara again under the guise of child visitation. He didn't see Lexie more than once a month before Melanie left him. And so Clara started losing weight, maybe so she'd look better when the two of them stand out on the porch discussing "childcare issues" for long stretches of time. I want to tell her that he's been putting irons in the fire all over town—I hear things—but I know how that might sound. All I want is for everything to be back to normal. And maybe the money can push it that way.

So when I walk in the house this morning, I'm searching for the smell of breakfast. It's a weekday, and weekdays are eggs and bacon days. Clara fries the slab bacon first, and then cooks the eggs in the grease and makes fresh coffee, percolated, none of this drip stuff.

And there's always plenty of buttered toast on the table, and a gallon of milk. I'm hungry just thinking about it.

But when I turn the corner and see Clara sitting at the table alongside Lexie it's obvious that things, today, are different. They've got empty cereal bowls in front of them. And Clara's all done up.

They look up but don't say anything, and it's as if they've stopped for me and posed. "Morning, ladies," I say.

"Morning, Lance," says Clara, and goes back to the puzzle she's working on with Lexie.

"Morning, Lance," says Lexie.

The smell of fresh soap has replaced the smell of bacon grease, and I don't know which question to ask first. "No eggs this morning?" I say.

"I'll make 'em if you want," says Clara. "We already had our breakfast."

"What's with the cereal?"

"What's wrong with cereal?" she says, and just as I'm about to tell her, she says, "You're late today."

"I went for a little drive," I say, and sit down, right away feeling guilty. I've got this ticket in my pocket that is the biggest thing that'll happen in our lives, and I'm keeping it a secret because all I can think about is why she's acting and looking the way she is. "That a new outfit?" I ask.

"It is."

"Going some place today?"

Clara looks at me as if I'm probing where I shouldn't. "Just work."

She works down at the diner. She's never worn a new pants suit to work as long as I've known her, and I wonder if Rob Foster is going to be in there today for lunch like he was a few days ago when I was driving by and just happened to see him sitting, of course, at one of Clara's tables; but I don't say anything.

Clara gets up and starts making breakfast. I turn to Lexie and ask her, "How you doing, honey?"

"Good," she says, and with a look beyond her years, asks, "Lance, why do you work the overnight shift all the time?"

"Eight percent more," I say.

"Eight percent more what?"

"Eight percent more money for doing the same job. It adds up."

But Lexie's little bluebell eyes are wanting more of an explanation; as if money isn't good enough. Lexie's more like me, I think, than like her mother and one of these days she's gonna stop calling me Lance and start calling me Daddy, I can feel it. She knows why I work at night, I've told her before when she's asked, and it's not because of the money. I say to her now, "I work at night because I like the daytime—I don't want to be cooped up in a factory all day long."

"But you're cooped up there all night," she says.

"That's different," I say, and wonder how I can adequately put it into words. "It's like... something going on when the rest of the town sleeps; something good. And I like the quiet when I go in and come out. And when I take my break, I go outside and look up at the sky." I look at her to see if I've lost her. "The stars are everywhere. I saw the sun rise this morning when I got out from work. How many people can say that?"

"All you have to do is wake up early," she says, soberly, and before I can really read anything into it, the phone rings and Clara jumps from her spot at the stove to get it, like she doesn't want anyone else to get it first.

So I grab the paper and take my customary seat at the table and listen for who it might be. Just as I'm about to take a sip of coffee, Clara calls out, "Oh my God, Lance!

Someone in Timber won the million dollar ticket!"

"A million dollars?!" says Lexie.

Before I can say anything, she's asking whoever's on the other end of the phone—Janie Mercier, her best friend, I'm sure—if they know who it is. Clara's nose is crinkled and she's having trouble rolling up her sleeves. She holds the phone between her neck and shoulder like she always does and squawks for another minute or two before hanging up the phone. She doesn't even take a breath before she blurts out, "There's a guy in town from the lottery. He's been staying at the motel, waiting for someone to win. The ticket was bought this morning at Mel's." Her eyes are a mix of excitement and dread, hoping, I'm sure, the ticket doesn't get into the wrong hands—which, in a small town like this means just about anyone except your own family.

Clara knows that I buy the occasional ticket, but why she doesn't ask me if I'd bought one today, I don't know. If she had asked me, I might have told her. What she does say to me is, "You don't even look surprised."

"Why should I be?" I say. "Someone had to win it, why not here in Timber?" I smile, hoping she'll catch on.

"It's just like you," she says and shakes her head, and

for the life of me I don't know what it is that's just like me, but she's been saying things like this lately. Do you have to always do that? she said yesterday, which I found out pertained to me sucking my teeth, something I didn't even know I did. And so I say now, "What's just like me?"

"That you wouldn't care about such a thing."

"Money?" I ask.

"Yes, money. You don't have it in you to make money."

"That money wasn't made, Clara. It was won."

She doesn't know what to say about that, so she says, "I bet you Rob won it."

I look at her for a moment. "That's an awfully strange thing to say."

"Oh yeah? Why?"

"Because of all the people in Timber, why would you immediately just call out his name?"

"Because maybe he wants something from life."

"Something that's not fat?" I say, and regret it the moment it's out of my mouth.

"What's that supposed to mean?" she says.

"I see the new you," I say, and she knows exactly what I mean.

"All you care about, Lance, is simple things."

"You're not simple," I say.

She looks at me, trying to determine if that's an insult or not.

This is getting out of hand. I say, "It's not what it looks like—"

"Save it, Lance. Save it."

***

I usually go to bed after breakfast in the morning and sleep until three or four in the afternoon. That gives me a few hours to do whatever I want until I'm expected back at the mill at six. But today, I don't feel like sleeping. The fight with Clara wasn't good and I had it in my mind that I'd apologize after I had a shower.

So after my shower I called out to her, but there was no reply. She and Lexie must have gone out somewhere; my guess is to snoop around and find out who won the money.

I get dressed in a nice turtleneck and corduroys and put on a little cologne, which isn't something I wear very often, and head out to find them. We only have one car, a Delta 88. It's the most comfortable vehicle I've ever been in. The interior is plush and faded cherry red, especially those spots that had been sat on for years or were there to be squeezed or turned or were just plain hit by the sun. It's a car that's not supposed to be good for Maine's snowy winter roads, but if you're from here you'd know how to get around with it just fine. Those people from out-of-state always seem to be driving an SUV of some sort, which is fairly ridiculous to me, seeing where most of them are from.

I love taking my rides, but now it's hard to enjoy it. I'm wondering if I should just tell Clara about the ticket and get this over with; but I can't help but think that that would defeat the purpose of our being together.

It's not until I see a crowd of people outside Mel's Convenience that I realize keeping my ticket secret may be more difficult than I suspected. The woman, Earlene, who works behind the counter, has a memory like an elephant. You stop in there just once and she'll remember how you like your coffee, and it was she that sold me the ticket this morning. My only hope is that because Mel's is just outside the plant, at shift change there are dozens of folks going in and out of there buying coffee and the paper, and a lot of people are buying scratch tickets, too.

I see Clara standing outside the store alongside some older Timber women, who are rough and more like men than they'd care to admit, and who are prototypes for what Clara will look like some day, at least pieces of them: a billy-goat hair on a chin here; short, easy-to-keep gray hair there; and, of course, the bulk that's been added to their frames one fried roll at a time. Lexie is standing beside them and looking around like she always does, so inquisitively, and I wonder what she's looking for. When she sees me, we lock eyes and there's a hint of a smile on her face, one of those sad smiles that I have a hard time deciphering. She continues to watch me, and I'm tempted to pull in, but I pass by. I'll head over to Charlie's Tavern to have a beer and figure out what the heck I should do.

Charlie's is a Timber institution. Part social club, part therapist's office the way things are discussed in there, though the patrons wouldn't think of it that way, of course. Everyone calls it The Moose because it has a big stuffed moose inside it. Not just the head on the wall or something, but the entire moose. Massive creature and so ugly it's beautiful. And the bar inside is the same one since the place opened, which is nearly fifty years now. The old-growth wood cut from our own forest is soft and smooth and pungent, in a good way, and your mug sinks into it a little bit when you put it down. Before I even open the door to the place, I can smell the sweet fermented yeast.

There's only about six of us, but I see Rob right away. He's the biggest man in the bar, wide in the shoulders and curly black hair on his head. He looks over, but doesn't acknowledge me, which is no different than the way it was back in high school when he was breaking records in hockey and I was sitting in the stands watching.

"What ya say, Lance?" says Gerry, the bartender. He's got a big red nose and the hint of an affected Irish brogue he'd picked up somewhere along the way.

"Hey, Gerry."

"Y'hear the news?"

" 'bout the lottery?"

"Million bucks. Someone's life is gonna change, I'd say."

"I'd say you're right."

I take the seat farthest away from Rob and my beer's already waiting for me. Ordinarily, the first sip would be pure delight, the way Gerry chills the mugs and how the beer is kept extra cold so that it crackles at the back of your throat when you drink it; but there's that Rob.

Everyone gets to talking about the lottery ticket and the things that type of money would buy. Rob is boisterous, as usual, but even a bit more so today, and I'm sure that's because I'm there. When people are feeling guilty they go out of their way to make it seem like they've got nothing to be guilty about. He's drinking heavily, I can see it in his eyes, and he's saying how if he was the one who won that money the first thing he'd do is leave this shit-hole town. There were a few nods at that.

"Piece a ass, that man's gonna get," says Raeford, who works beside me on the line.

"How you know it's a man?" says Gerry.

"I don't, but if it's a damn woman, she can get herself a piece a ass, too—mine."

Everyone laughs at that.

"Man, if I had that ticket," says Jeffy. "Goddamn I'd be out of here, too."

"Yeah?" says Raeford, amused. "Where would you go?"

Jeffy shrugga his shoulders. "I don't know...Florida."

"You been to Florida?" saya Raeford.

"No."

"Well how do you know you want to go to Florida then, dipshit?"

"How do I know I don't?"

We all laugh some more. Their bickering continues for a while, with everyone getting a few quips in here and there, until Gerry cries out, "Look!" He points to the TV on the wall. "The news is outside Mel's!"

On the TV is a crowd and a reporter interviewing the guy from the lottery, who looks like one of those stiff, Portland types. "All I can say is this: whoever won that ticket hasn't come forward yet. Maybe they don't know they've won, I don't know." He looks into the camera and says, "If you bought a ticket today and haven't scratched it yet, you might want to think about doing it now."

"What type of ying-yang does he think we are?" says Gerry. "Everyone who buys scratch tickets, that's the first thing they do is scratch it."

"Nobody waits!" shouts someone behind the Lottery guy, and everyone laughs, even him.

"Okay, so does anyone know who the winner is?" the reporter asks the crowd. The camera scans the faces of people we all know, and it's more like watching a home movie than the news. A camera crew hasn't been in Timber for years, probably since Tim Duquesne got crushed in the wood stripper at the plant. The camera pans a bit and I look for Clara and Lexie, and there they are, just off to the side but in full view. I look over to Rob right away and he's done the very same thing; our eyes lock, but it's only his that look away.

Sitting on my stool, I feel the world spinning. There's a sickness in my stomach. I don't know exactly what it's from. A bunch of things, I guess. The lottery isn't really something I wanted; I was hoping for fifty bucks, maybe, to buy an outfit for Lexie or Clara, maybe a night out at China Garden over in Williston Falls. But the more I think of it, the more I see that that's not the problem. The problem's Clara. It's what she's thinking about more than what she's feeling. It wasn't but a day before the news came out about Rob and Melanie breaking up that she looked me in the eyes and said after we'd made love that I was the best thing to ever happen to her in her entire life and she couldn't wait to get up out of bed in the morning to greet me when I came home, so we could eat that nice breakfast together and do the little things we do.

What exactly she's got in her head now, who the hell knows, except it has to do with that dipshit Rob, who's surely helping things along; and while I'd be justified to take a swing at him, it's just as much Clara's fault. She can't see that whether they were having an affair or not he'd leave her high and dry if he had that million dollars. I may not know many things in life, but I know people, and I know Rob and there he is getting up from his stool, drunkenly, heading to the bathroom, and suddenly it all makes sense.

I follow him in. He's standing at the urinal. I go and stand next to him. But instead of taking a leak, I take the ticket out of my pocket. I don't say a word, just put it right there on top of his urinal so that he can see it, and I walk out.

I finish my beer and leave the bar and head straight for the pay phone in the parking lot. I look in the phone book and get channel 10's phone number and call it. I tell whoever answers the phone, "I've got news about who won that lottery. His name is Rob Foster. He's at the Moose and he's waiting for you."

I wait around for a bit, just to see the news truck fly into the lot, followed by the mass of people rushing over excitedly from Mel's. That was all I could do. I go on home to wait.

***

At home, we've got this sectional; a nice one that two people can lie on at the same time without even touching. Sometimes it's best that way. You can be together but separate, not right up on top of each other. I lay down on it and try to take a nap. The repeat of last night's Bruins game is on TV, and I've got to say there's nothing more relaxing than closing your eyes and listening to the sweet voice of Johnny Bucyk doing the Bruins' play-by-play. His voice is deep and throaty and because he was a former player he always has these little insights that a regular person just wouldn't know. And it's that that I love; that there's so many layers to a simple thing like men moving up and down the ice with sticks and a puck. I concentrate hard on what he's saying, trying to keep my mind off what's happening at the bar and whether I know human nature as well as I think I do.

An hour or so passes before the door opens, and I hear Clara and Lexie's voices. I close my eyes and make like I'm sleeping, and when they see me they get real quiet. Lexie goes off to her room to play and Clara comes and sits down on the couch. I don't say anything, just keep my eyes closed. She's looking at me, I can sense it. After a bit she gets up and goes to the kitchen and rummages around in the cabinets and comes back crinkling a bag of chips. She sits back down, and through half-open eyes I watch her eating. The chips are the kind I always buy, full-fat Lays. She hasn't touched them in weeks, but now she's got her whole fist in the bag. She crunches down and chews and chews like she hasn't had a meal in ages. Her fingers glisten with oil and when they reach a maximum grease level, she licks them and goes back for more.

This goes on for a while. With each bite she seems to get more ravenous, and I wonder exactly how it happened down at the bar. If Rob got on his bus right then, or if Melanie somehow found out and went and sat down on his lap, or if Clara just plain realized she was expendable. It doesn't really matter, because every so often, when I stir, Clara rubs my leg like she used to and I wonder how it feels.

Piles

From behind his old wood desk in his suburban Portland home, Thurston Brunt looked back on his childhood in a little western Maine town called Cassolis with the oddest regret. He hadn't been back since his parents had passed away within days of each other, and even then it had been several years since the previous time he had been there. He hadn't wanted to expose his children.

Now, his father was a complexity in his mind, standing with his hands on his hips contemplating those piles of junk. Why had he never expanded the lot? The offer to purchase the land next door had been made a dozen times by Mr. Rasmussen, always below market. He could see the question in Rasmussen's eyes, Who was a junk dealer with just a quarter-acre lot?

So instead of some form of manageable organization, exploding out of the ground were tremendous jagged piles of rust and rubber and cracked varnished wood. Three piles, his babies.

But was his father what that woman had said? She was from away and had stopped to take pictures. She asked him right in front his wife and two boys if he was a junk artist. A what? A junk artist. He glanced over at the three of them then back at the woman, looking as if he wanted to kick her teeth right down her throat. He made no reply at all.

But what else could it be? There was that special ladder he had constructed of odd bits of metal, bolted together with thick screws that he had brushed with a special machine to make them scuffed and shiny. The ladder was slightly crooked this way and that, the way it might be in Dr. Seuss, and he would lean it up against a pile and climb, stopping here or there for whatever item he had decided upon. Up he would go, and down he would come. If it was morning he would carry whatever it was—an old aluminum kitchen chair, some rare hubcap, a winter tire with no match—to the side of the road for that day's advertisement; and then he would go back for more, deliberating, his thick, hairless hands on his hips as he studied, sometimes for a half hour or more before climbing back up and reaching for something else. If what he wanted was in the middle of the pile he would spend hours taking down everything on top of it, not the least bit discouraged, relishing the opportunity to load it all back up again, taking his time, doing it in some different order before stepping back and having a look. But what had he seen, standing there staring? Why hadn't he seen the hunger on their faces?

The only time he seemed to notice them was the one day a month he drove down into Farmington in his rickety old truck with the trailer he had fashioned himself. When sundown came he'd be back, licorice for them as an afterthought, barely able to hide his excitement with his little treasures, an assortment of sinks and carburetors and lamps. He would stay up all night in the back, floodlights on, climbing up, sometimes stopping to stare up into the sky before fixing and arranging, climbing back down, stepping back, then up again to remove an item, place it somewhere else, staring, under the moon looking very much like what he was, a potato farmer's boy all grown up in his overalls and boots, except that was no crop he was obsessed with.

His mother offered no clue. She would sometimes look out the back window at her husband and his piles, but there was never so much as a shrug. She wasn't looking to see if there was anything in them. To her, he was just a junk dealer and those were just his piles.

Carolyn had asked him about his parents on their first date in Portland. He'd told her they were dead. It was a year before he confessed they weren't. He told her about the piles. "That says a lot about you," Carolyn had said, and she hadn't meant it meanly. "Was it painful?" she asked. Like his father would have, he wanted to kick her teeth right down her throat. But he was an accountant in Portland now. Carolyn dropped it, except every once in a while, when the kids weren't around, she might find a way to bring it up.

And so there he was in business for himself, behind his desk, staring out the window at his expansive lawn all flat and brown, wondering whether or not his father was what that lady had said, some type of junk artist; and just waiting, it seemed, for when Carolyn would find some way to bring the whole thing up again.

and the imitation flagstone patio. And then there was the shed, as big as a little house. It had a four-paned window with a flower box beneath it and a nice wide door.

Listen. Fuck it. When it came to Saturday and Sunday you could do whatever it was you wanted out there. Jeanine was the one who'd wanted the shed in the first place, because if you were going to drink like that then at least you could do it out of the neighbors' sight. If you're gonna drink those things, she'd said, then do it inside the shed. What those things were were margaritas. You had a little kit furnished from teak, with one compartment for salt that you'd rim the glasses with such beautiful care. That kit and those glasses were kept in such good shape, like everything inside the shed, and like almost nothing outside it. Unlike outside, inside was small and easy to control and when you were there, like you were for most of the days and even the nights on Saturdays and Sundays, you had so much time to keep things orderly, and Jeanine didn't mind, God bless her soul, she'd told you to get it, and now she had her house and you had yours, and she was no angel either, not that she had any vices she was hiding, but she understood you, had grown up down the hall from you, and she knew what it was like to have your brother shot before your eyes, she'd been there to see it.

But that's not why you drank. There were other reasons, too. Like you, Jeanine had grown up listening to the music blaring out the windows all over the projects on Saturday mornings, the hungover fathers and grandfathers listening to Gerry McGorvey's Saturday morning Irish music show on AM 560. That was just drink. And this you could control. The shed. The shelves ordered with drawers with things for work projects that might someday get done. The Ball glass jars on one side, polished and clear and bright. You put little things in them, like certain size nails and screws. A fan for days like this when the devil was breathing his hell. And you could sit in this great wood chair, antique and refinished by a real live woodworker, a craftsman who'd smiled when you'd said you needed a good drinking chair.

And you sit in the chair. And you stand. And all the shelves with stuff so nicely ordered on them. And the Ball glass jars. The screws. The nails. All of a certain size. A chest with drawers. That little teak kit. Turn up the radio. Sit down in the chair. Stand up. Wander around the backyard, the one you'd dreamed about when you

It's Time to Die

Okay already, let's just make it time to die. I am forty. I am a believer in the good Lord, God and in Jesus Christ, His only Son, who died on the cross for my sins and the sins of mankind. So, why not?

I have told my wife, "Life is like a prolonged finals week, don't you just want to be on summer vacation?"

She has always replied, "God gave us this life not just to die, but to live."

"That's true," I said one time, "but Jesus was only thirty-three."

"Moses was over a hundred" was her answer.

I almost told her that I have always found that hard to believe—because why would I, if I believed all of the other stuff?—but I just kept my trap shut.

I go on living, of course. And no, nothing is so bad: American. Or maybe it's too, too bad: American, or just human.

But anyway, no one can see inside my mind where I wonder, still, *Why can't it just be time to die?*

Acknowledgments

A special thank you to my mother and father, the most selfless people I know. And to all those writers along the way, especially Janette van Gruisen, who encouraged me and challenged me and helped me to be the writer I am today.